God's Country Club

Also by Gail Donohue Storey

The Lord's Motel

God's
Country Club

a novel

Gail Donohue Storey

PERSEA BOOKS   NEW YORK

ACKNOWLEDGMENTS

For their insight and support I am grateful to my editor, Karen Braziller; my publisher, Michael Braziller; and my agent, Ellen Levine, as well as to Jacqueline Damian, Porter Storey, M.D., and my family. I would also like to thank my irrepressible research team: Ann, Carla, Colleen, Grace, Holly, Kelli, Kenny, Lise, Marjie, Mary, and Phyllis.

God's Country Club *is a work of fiction. Names, characters, and events in this book are the product of the author's imagination. Places are used fictitiously. Any similarity to actual events or real persons, living or dead, is entirely coincidental and not intended by the author.*

Persea Books, Inc.
171 Madison Avenue
New York, New York 10016

Library of Congress Cataloging-in-Publication Data

Storey, Gail Donohue.
    God's country club : a novel / by Gail Donohue Storey.
    p. cm.
    Sequel to: The Lord's motel.
    ISBN 0-89255-219-0 (hardcover : alk. paper)
    1. Man-woman relationships—Texas—Fiction. 2. Single women—Texas—Fiction. 3. Houston (Tex.)—Fiction. I. Title.
    PS3569.T6487G63   1996
    813'.54—dc20   96-14744
                                                                            CIP

Typeset in Sabon by Keystrokes, Lenox, Massachusetts
Manufactured in the United States of America
First Edition

For Dr. Storey

CONTENTS

God's Country Club

1

Fried Different Vegetable Together

Gabriel's condo complex is called God's Country Club, but the landscape service went belly-up and only the cactus survive. Moving in with him today, I make my way through the prickly pear around the clubhouse and pool. We've just stored most of my belongings in the Buffalo Mini-Warehouses. Everyone in Houston has a past life in a mini-warehouse. I come from the ranks of the sexually anxious, but Gabriel makes my soul sigh with relief.

At the door of his condo, he picks me up and carries me over the threshold. His apartment is new, post-divorce. With its arched white ceilings and skylights, it looks like a church without pews. My heart broke when I first saw it and his pared-down existence: one spatula from Wal-Mart, towels newly monogrammed with only his initials, sleeping bag, nested camping pans and bowls. It was the highest quality camping equipment, but still. He was traveling too lightly, as if living on a boat, with a Japanese economy of space. Instead of a sofa, there was a canoe in his living room. "I want to share my furniture with you," I said.

He loves me so much he won't put me down. He's not

what I'd call a romantic, just given to manly heroics. We're kissing in his arms, my legs dangling, when the phone in my pocket rings. He gave me my cellular phone so I could page him anytime, anywhere, but neither of us expected it to backfire on us like this.

"Tell me everything," Gigi says on the other end. "Did he make room in his closet?"

Gabriel holds me so close, my phone between his shoulder and my ear, that for a moment I think Gigi's asking whether he makes love in his closet.

"I can't talk now, Gigi," I say. Gigi's my oldest living friend. She and I came to Houston from Boston during the great Yankee yuppie migration, and until this morning I lived across the hall from her in the Lord's Motel.

"Just answer yes or no," she says. "Is he standing right there?"

"Yes."

"Does he have an erection?"

"Gigi!"

"Yes or no?"

Gabriel puts me down. I pray it wasn't because he overheard the e-word.

I sneak a peak so Gigi will get off my back. "Sort of."

"Sort of!" she says. "No such thing as sort of in this matter."

"I have to go now, Gigi." I can't just hang up on her because men come and go, but women friends are forever. If we chose men the way we choose our women friends, the world would be a different place.

"I love you," Gabriel mouths. To make up for putting me down, he folds me into his arms. In his armadillo cowboy boots, he's so tall his chin touches the top of my head at my seventh chakra.

I turn my face toward his blond beard and feel the raised blue letters of his monogrammed doctor's coat imprint on my cheek: Gabriel Benedict, M.D. But being held by the most gorgeous man on the planet while listening to Gigi is giving me an instant dissociative personality disorder.

"Listen to me very carefully, Colleen," she says. "Once you move in with a man, the timebomb starts ticking toward the nanosecond when he decides whether he wants to marry you. You miss that nanosecond and you're toast."

"When is it?" I say. I'm terrified, but Gabriel should be too. What about the nanonsecond when I decide whether I want to marry him?

"You know not the day nor the hour," she says. "Years from now, or by dinner. I'll call you back in five minutes."

I press the End button and look at Gabriel's altimeter watch, but even it doesn't have nanoseconds.

"This watch is waterproof to thirty meters," Gabriel says.

"Where are we going that deep?"

He looks into my eyes. When I first met him he was standing under a bright light in the hospital emergency room. It was as if God were pointing him out to me.

"Let's celebrate your moving in by going out to dinner," he says.

"Shouldn't I try out your kitchen?" I ought to start right away on my audition. My furniture's in storage, but not my pots and pans.

He kisses me, then looks at me even more inscrutably. We've been dating for a year, but he has a lavish repertoire of feelings he leaves completely to my imagination. With most quiet people you'd like to think still waters run deep but you're afraid not. Gabriel, on the other hand, makes a metaphysic out of everything. The main thing we have in common is obsessing on the world's problems. I play them out on the personal level, while be broods about how to solve them.

"I miss you," I say. His mysteriousness makes me anxious. I'm so convinced by his silence that he wants out of the relationship, it's as if he's already gone.

"I'm standing right here." He envelops me with his broad shoulders, powerful arms. It's too bad most men don't get to feel enveloped, but then, they probably wouldn't like it.

Through the starchy smell of his doctor's coat, I inhale his musky warmth.

"Your hair is like Spanish moss," he says, and strokes it. Outdoorsy men like Gabriel think that's a compliment. Maybe my henna is rusting. My hair is long and curly, but I'd better try a new conditioner.

He answers the dinner question by holding the door open for me. One of the things I love about Gabriel is he gives me what I want before I know I want it.

"You're wearing your doctor's coat out to dinner?" I say.

"It's my favorite coat."

He's too considerate to ask me to leave my phone at home. It's weird to think of his condo as home. I guess this means we'll be seeing a lot more of each other. Maybe I should get a pedicure since he'll be seeing even my feet more now.

We go out and climb into his Ford pickup, with its gun rack, mud flaps, bumper stickers. He borrowed the truck from his family's ranch when Felicity got the house with the two-car garage, both cars, and their son in the divorce. The pickup is custom-painted black and white, brindled like a cow, with a longhorn hood ornament. It mortifies Gabriel to drive it, but I'm trying to get him to enter it in the Art Car Parade.

We drive down Buffalo Speedway. There aren't any buffalo in Houston, just DINKs and yuppies stampeding to Whole Paycheck Market. We pass the mini-warehouse where my stuff is stored.

"Must be hard to leave behind your old life at the Lord's Motel," he says.

"Not as hard as you might think." It rather feels as if Gigi is making sure my old life comes right along with me. "But I miss my waterbed."

"I'm not critical of your taste," he says. "It's what one is expected to do in it."

"What do you have in mind?"

"Nothing that can't be done on my new futon."

"It was a fun bed. Now I've got the man but not the bed."

"I'm not a fun guy."

"You have potential."

He brightens, but like a votive candle rather than a red light on lower Westheimer. He's a serious person, but not depressed. I really don't have that much to be depressed about, but when did that ever stop anyone? If I were happier, I might be able to cope with someone as serious as Gabriel. Already I'm a ton happier from moving in with him, but if it doesn't work out I'll be so depressed I'll never recover.

It's one of those steamy June evenings when the air hangs heavy and green, ripe for lightning to ignite it in sheets. I have this foreboding that Gabriel's going to make me encounter myself. Would I like being more real? Authenticity is the booby prize we get for existentialism.

We pull into a parking place at the Asian Kitchen. Gabriel comes around to open the pickup door. He walks with the restrained swagger of a man who's comfortable being large but doesn't want to hurt anyone with it.

"I'll change seats with you," I say, as soon as we've been seated.

"I'm okay."

"No you're not." I get up and stand by his chair.

He reluctantly moves over to my chair, brings his already unfolded napkin. He's not afraid of anything but sitting with his back to the door. "It's okay to live dangerously now and then," he says. He reaches for my hand across the table.

"Why worry about something you don't have to when there are so many other things to worry about?" I say. Worry is how organized people like me take care of their catastrophes in advance. My plan to marry him is a catastrophe in the making. I'm helplessly attracted to his goodness, his self-confidence, his competence.

"Like what?"

"You could get killed in gang crossfire in the emergency room."

He's in charge of the emergency room at the county hospital, where the staff can't keep up with Houston's tragedies. He puts in long hours of overtime, just to keep the E.R. open. He impales himself on the work ethic.

"The hospital just installed metal detectors," he says. "What are you afraid of?"

"The mugger."

"What mugger?"

I study the menu. The best thing about being a vegetarian is it telescopes big, plastic foldout menus into a half-dozen choices. Mugger is code for the rapist women have to watch out for. We've been raised with three categories of fear: not getting married, nuclear holocaust, and the rapist. Not getting married and the rapist are two sides of one fear.

"Should we get some spring rolls?" I say.

"You can handle anything," he says. "You've driven back

and forth across America several times by yourself in a car that was falling apart, been through fires, famine, and pestilence, and are sitting here without a scratch, having dinner with me."

"You haven't seen my psychological scars."

"Badges of honor."

Gabriel is both horrified at what he already knows about me and fascinated I've survived. It's like his fascination for the E.R.'s demimonde, emotional counterpoint to his aristocratic background. The lower the class, the bigger the emergency, while people as rich as his family take their crises to the bank.

"Are you worried what your parents would think of my waterbed?"

"When would they see it?"

"Soon. You told me your mother likes to get involved."

"We won't invite her into the bedroom."

"That's the first place she'll check when she comes to visit."

We've assiduously avoided introducing each other to our families until our relationship is more assured. His mother and my father have a lot to do with why we're the way we are, but neither of us is ready to have that dramatically demonstrated. It's one thing to console each other for the way we were raised, but another to see how intractable the resulting personality flaws are going to prove.

"How are you going to introduce me to your parents if they just show up?"

"You're my POSSLQ, and I'm yours," he says. "Persons of Opposite Sex Sharing Living Quarters, as the Census Bureau puts it."

"That's all?"

"Now that we live together, we ought to visit your parents in Boston. They'll want to know I come from a good Texas family, have been educated at the best schools, have money, and am a person of good repute."

"Why don't we just send them your curriculum vitae?"

I already know that his parents had him baptized three times by various Protestant denominations, his father will never sell his mineral rights, and his mother's flatware pattern is Grand Baroque. Gabriel knows I grew up in a housing project, my father is now residentially challenged, and my mother does her spring cleaning in February.

"I'd like the Fried Different Vegetable Together," I say, reading it off the menu.

The waiter takes our order—Moo-Shoo Tofu in addition to the Fried Different. "Brown rice or white?" he says.

"Brown rice is harder on the kidneys because it takes more water to digest," I say after we've ordered the brown. "But that doesn't worry me."

"Good, because that's not how the kidneys work."

When the waiter brings our spring rolls, Gabriel cuts his in two and pours peanut sauce into both halves. They're served on thick plastic plates exquisitely colored with oriental designs and must have come from a Wal-Mart in Beijing.

"I'll never make you sit with your back to the door," I say. "What's that about?"

"Not sitting with my back to the mouth of the cave."

"Maybe you were stabbed in the back in a former life."

"Maybe I'll be stabbed in the back by a former wife."

The waiter brings our tofu and Fried Different Vegetable Together.

I feel a stab of love as I watch him eat. He wraps his arm around his plate, like a caveman protecting his food. He makes even this gesture look like good manners. I love how he's both primitive male and Texan aristocrat. His absorption in his food is so complete, so perfect, I'm pierced by the desire to take care of him for the rest of his life. I want to protect him and his food from dinosaurs, wolves, his ex-wife, gangs, his mother.

"Web never slept in that waterbed," I say. "If that's what you're worried about."

Web, my previous boyfriend, loved kinky sex so much I got arrested for prostitution. The social director on a cruise ship, he persuaded me to do an exotic dance for a bachelor party in Galveston. I'm a librarian, but I took public service too far. I didn't go through with the prostitution part, but it took Gabriel the whole year of our dating to come to terms with the aspersions cast on my character.

"I'm not worried about Web or my parents," he says. "I'm concerned about how Gabe will adjust to our living together. Men get nervous when women move the furniture."

Gabe is Gabriel and Felicity's two-year-old. I've met him, but he pretends I'm not there by relating exclusively to Gabriel. Some kids have an imaginary friend; Gabe has me for his imaginary enemy. Does Gabriel really think Gabe won't notice I'm there if the furniture's the same?

"When he visits," I say, "I'll go sleep on my bed in the mini-warehouse."

"Let's not argue about it."

"Sorry." Love is always having to say you're sorry.

"I feel guilty I left Gabe."

I'd tell him how much worse it was when my father left me, but he'd only feel worse about Gabe. He can't separate his love for Gabe from the pain. What he wants is impossible: for me to be a kinder, gentler Felicity, and for us to have a perfected version of his flawed marriage.

"We can't be one little happy family," I say, "you, Gabe, Felicity, and me. I can't graft myself on like that." What I want is equally impossible, for Felicity and Gabe to disappear, for Gabriel and me to start all over. It won't work; I'm in recovery from my own family.

"It's a tragic situation all around," Gabriel says. "But I love you." He sticks his elbow out, turns his hand around on his thigh, leans on it. Texan men do that, as if ready to saddle up. It's a man's version of a woman putting her hand on her hip.

"I love you too."

He spreads plum sauce on a flour pancake, loads it with vegetables, rolls it up, and offers it to me.

"You have it," I say.

"I'll make mine next."

His sudden tenderness knocks me off balance even as it reassures me of his love. Where I come from, every crisis means the end. But he defends me from my own self-accusations.

My cellular phone rings again. "This is Houston, do you read me?" Gigi says. "Every woman in this city is waiting for your support."

"Report?" I say.

"If you won't bring in Gabriel for yourself, do it for our networking group," Gigi says. "He's the contact we need to every straight, single, male doctor in the Texas Medical Center."

"I can't believe this," I say.

"They're talking Woman of the Year," she says. "Think what it would mean to your career."

Gabriel ladles brown rice onto my plate, covers it with tantalizing spoonfuls of tofu and shiitake mushrooms. Is it my imagination, or is he beginning to temper the love in his eyes with a teensy bit of impatience?

"What's bothering Gigi she has to call you so much?" he says when I press End again.

"Work," I say. "Work is all she ever thinks about."

He looks unconvinced, although work is all he ever thinks about, except for Gabe and me. He picks up my chopsticks, puts them in my hand, folds my fingers over them. "Colleen," he says, "let's eat our dinner before it gets cold."

I eat and listen to him talk about his day—drug crises, gunshot wounds, suicides, teenage mothers giving birth in the waiting room. His deep blue eyes flash with the luminosity of the aurora borealis, draw me into their magnetic field. He works his chopsticks as if probing for bullets, sewing sutures.

What will it take for me to shift from a shame-based to a love-based sexual economy? It's not that I think I'm not lovable. You can believe you're lovable all you want, but if someone else doesn't think so, what difference does it make? Men have loved me for selective reasons, but Gabriel's the first to love the whole package.

Now that I'm living with the man I love, maybe for the rest of my life, I want to make love right. But what does that mean? Sex with Web was a performance—all spectacle and pageantry, exotic dancing and role-playing. I'm not sure I've ever had sex when I wasn't someone else. What if I can't make love as myself? When Gabriel and I made love before we lived together, it was fine because it wasn't going anywhere. I try to remember what that was like, but all I can think of is the nanosecond.

"Is our generation obsessed with sexual pleasure to make up for our fears for the future of the planet?" I ask.

"Sex is great, but I'm not obsessed with it."

"You have more meaning in your life than most people," I say.

He likes to make love to me, but he doesn't like to *play,*

particularly. He doesn't want to do anything that would countermand his dignity as a man and a human being. Not to mention he'd be embarrassed to play in a world so full of global and personal tragedy.

He turns on the overhead fan to cool our steamy bodies. He looks twice his size in half his clothes, his hairy chest a vast expanse, his legs as long as trees. His sculpted muscles are dusted with hair as blond as sand. How can I use my overwhelming desire for him to satisfy my longing?

"Don't do anything with me you don't want to do," he says.

"It's not that I don't want to do it," I say. "I'm just a little conflicted. Can you work with me on that?"

"Sure," he says. "But we can't work on it *all* the time. Sometimes we'll work on it, other times we'll make love for the fun of it."

"Then we're really on the same side."

"Of what?" he asks. He smiles so tenderly, then pulls me to him.

I may be bad, but with him I believe in my own goodness.

2

Soon as I Get Myself Together

Gabriel has left for the E.R. by the time I wake up at dawn. What time must someone have to get up to have an emergency and already be at the hospital for it? Or is Gabriel solving crises left over from the night before?

I eat breakfast and get ready for work, then head out of the God's Country Club parking lot in my red VW bug. The bug is too light to activate the automatic security gate. I hop out and jump up and down on the sensor. What should I tell my family about moving in with Gabriel? The gate opens; I drive through just before it sweeps closed behind me. It's like narrowly avoiding a spanking.

Vanessa Jones, the new library director, wants to see me in her office the minute I get to work.

"Girlfriend," she says, "we've got a problem with the homeless."

Ms. Jones was appointed to bring the Houston library budget into the black. She has already got the branches delivering Service-to-the-Unserved, my outreach project to take library materials to prisoners and the homebound. I hope that doesn't mean I'll be downsized, because I'm looking forward to working with her. Brainy, statuesque, African-American, she'll be a different order of mentor.

"The homeless are big library users," I say. "They use it to keep warm, except in Houston where they use it to keep cool."

"That's a mandate from the homeless for library service."

"More air conditioners?"

"You're the queen of outreach," she says, and points a beautifully lacquered fingernail at me. "Whom do you suggest for outreach to the homeless?"

"Me?"

The queen of outreach is the daughter of homelessness; my own father is marginally homeless. He lives in a building in South Boston, abandoned since his landlady died. He had some sort of relationship with her, and now it's as if he's too grief-stricken to move on. Without my own apartment and with most of my stuff in storage, I'm one step from homelessness myself.

"You?" Vanessa says, and raises her eyebrows. "The streets are too dangerous for a woman. I was thinking of Ralph, the bookmobile librarian."

Ralph and I are on rival tracks for promotion to associate director. "I want to do it. I'll take self-defense."

"I was planning to make you associate director," she says, "with a large, attractive office next to mine. But if you insist."

I look down at the foot I shot myself in, then up again at Vanessa. "I have contacts in the homeless community." My father may be in Boston, but the real global community is the homeless one.

"Take them terminals to access our online services," she says. "We have to stay on the cutting edge of nonprint."

"They don't have anyplace to plug anything in."

"Let them read books."

"Some of them can't read, but we could teach them."

"Girl, homelessness is making a comeback," she says. "So is illiteracy. The cutting edge is a double-edged sword, and we may be able to do some good."

"I'll start yesterday."

"You have to do a study first."

"What kind of study?"

"Three hundred pages."

"The trustees won't wade through that, Ms. Jones."

"Call me Vanessa."

Houston's homeless have had a public relations problem ever since a homeless man stole the mayor's wife's rose bushes from in front of City Hall. Maybe the library can help.

In between my calls to two homeless shelters, Web calls from his cruise ship in the Caribbean. "Colleen," he says in his conspiratorial whisper, "come meet me in Aruba."

I've hardly thought of Web in the year I've been dating Gabriel, but now I see his wiry tanned body stretched out in a deck chair. His dark curls swim on his head, his emerald eyes shine; he has a white piña colada in his hand. Every date with Web was a party in one exotic place or another.

"I'm living with someone now."

"I don't mind."

"Gabriel would," I say. Gabriel will probably work in the E.R. all weekend. I've never been to Aruba.

"We'll swim and snorkel in the turquoise water," he goes on. "We'll have beach barbecues, treasure hunts, wild theme parties every night."

As a cruise director, Web's job is to get people to do things they don't want to, but in my case it was kinky sex instead of shuffleboard.

"And what else?" I say.

"Nothing more exciting than topless sunbathing on Bachelor's Beach, if you don't want to."

"I don't think so."

On my way to my first appointment at a dropouts' drop-in center, I get lost in a run-down part of downtown. I apologize to Georgia Balboni, the executive director, when I show up twenty minutes late.

"M'dear, I've been twenty minutes late all my life," she says.

About thirty men and a few women stand in line in front of the small office, a trailer on blocks. Mrs. Balboni floats on the front step like an aging Southern belle on the verandah. She writes down their names as each shows his meager identification.

"I forgot my Social Obscurity card," says one man who shuffles and scratches.

One desperate woman doesn't speak English. Mrs. Balboni enlists the aid of a Latino to translate. It's not clear what the woman wants—some kind of letter so she can go to the hospital.

"Ask her again," Mrs. Balboni says.

She gives the woman directions to a public health clinic, but the woman thinks she's being turned away. I want to run after her, sort it all out for her somehow, send her to Gabriel in the E.R.

"If we don't seem organized, it's because we're not," Mrs. Balboni says to me when we go inside to her tiny cubicle. "In crisis work you can't be organized. I'm organizationally impaired."

"What are your objectives?" I say. It's the first question for my study. I open up my laptop.

"We try to get them some clothes, haircuts, bus tokens to get to a job. We get them to clean their fingernails, we keep these people going."

The receptionist rushes in to whisper that one of the clients in the waiting room is freaking out. "He's using words," she says.

Mrs. Balboni sighs and takes the man outside.

I peek into the waiting room where the others doze and fidget. I'm struck by the sensuality of the homeless—sex, babies, body odor, hunger, caked dirt. Some are rolling in the ashes. Others try to escape the body totally, climbing the wisp of drug consciousness. Has my father looked for help in places like this? Everyone homeless is someone's family.

"I've never had any real trouble with the people who come here," Mrs. Balboni says when she comes back. "If they're crazy, I'm used to it. If they look troublemaking, I say, 'Let's go out back and have a little chat, away from all this.' We try and get these people back in the mainstream, but this is an unrealistic assumption in many cases. The streets are full of people who are somewhat nutty, probably thirty or forty percent of them."

"How did that happen?"

"Let me tell you something, honey. Back in the sixties, the best social work and medical thinking of the day said, 'Let these people out of the so-called snake pits—the state institutions—and let them return to warm, loving homes.' No one stopped to think where all the warm, loving homes were going to come from." She sits back as if I will tell her where.

"They're mentally ill?"

"We need as a culture to sit down and find out what in our society causes so much of it," she goes on. "The government is not coping, and it's too big a problem for the government, anyway. These are the people wandering the streets, shouting to the heavens all kinds of wild things, eating out of the dumpsters. They don't take their medication the way they should."

"Where do they get their medication?"

"Well, they can get it at the county hospital, the public health clinics, but they don't *do* it. The public views these people as lazy riffraff, but this is not the case. Some days they have a good day and we can put them in the labor pool. The next they have a bad day and they can't do a thing for anybody." She gazes out into the waiting room. "And now we've got drugs and everything else."

I explain the feasibility study I'm doing for library service for the homeless. "Can you introduce me to an exemplary homeless person to be a key subject and help me navigate the street?"

"There's your man," she says, and points to a young African-American. In the sea of agitated people, he studies the Help Wanted ads posted on the bulletin board. He looks vulnerable, worried.

"We don't want to imply this is an African-American problem," I say. "Would a Caucasian be more politically correct?"

"You don't want people of color to think you're ignoring them, either."

"It's going to get me coming and going."

"The trouble with political correctness," she says, "is it's not about the way things are but the way we're pushing them to go."

I struggle with the implications of this while Mrs. Balboni motions the man into her office. "I'm going to make an investment in you, Chance," she says to him. "I'm giving you some bus tokens and a few dollars for clothes you'll need for your job interviews."

"I don't want to take too much of your time, looking at what you got out there," Chance says, and tilts his head toward the waiting room. His thick Afro is dented from his Rockets cap. He's tall and lanky; his gray sweatshirt and sweatpants hang on his gaunt body.

"It's your turn. Keep coming back until we get you organized. And this young lady," she says, "needs your help if you'll say yes to reading." She ushers us to a corner of the waiting room. Her plastic beads rattle on her bosom as she walks away.

Chance and I look warily at each other, like two unhappy adolescents forced by our dancing teacher to fox-trot. His brown eyes dart away and back again. He may be homeless, but he's not the Mugger.

"Is Chance your street name?" I ask.

"My mother name me Chance for a rodeo cowboy got gored by a bull," he says. "You got a boyfriend?"

"Yes."

"You got any cocaine?"

"No."

" 'Caine started out with a good attitude, but it all boils down, they want something back before it's over with. By you being a woman, being new, we going to treat you the best way we do, make it real sweet. After that, I breaks you in, you belongs to me."

"I wouldn't think a woman who cared for you would want to live like that." I clutch my laptop. "Wouldn't she rather see you learn to read than help you maintain that lifestyle?"

"Well, if she love you, she stay with you, but she really

want you out of the drug lifestyle. She want out of it, because the woman's more sensitive. The man who's been in it a long time, he'll tell her, take big risks. A man is young and cocky, macho-like. Somebody sucker-punch him, suck him in, or if he sell people bad drugs, he walk out to the car and somebody snatch the drugs he had and blow his brains out."

"Chance," I say, "why are you homeless?"

"Why? I been asking myself the same question. When I first started out, I was married, for two years." He leans forward. "It wasn't drugs that broke the relationship, that I know. For me, I got sent away from here, I went to the state hospital and stayed down a month. I mixed with murderers, real sick psychiatric people. You know who the crazy people are?"

"Who?"

"The people out here," he says, "in reality. Let's say it that way. Why? Because the people locked up, in the nuthouse, is not as crazy, not as dumb, criticizing people."

"Everyone out here isn't crazy."

"If they open their eyes, give an individual person a chance, instead of accuse, before a judge, then the world be better off. I almost got my last ticket in my own home, by my own wife. That's my point. Me being innocent as I was, it's not I was heavy into drugs, it's just what I was going through at the time with the divorce."

My father blames his decline on my mother. "Your mother and I, honey, are two different birds of a feather." I hate it when he calls me honey. Did he call my mother that? No one, least of all my mother, could have coped with my father's drinking, gambling, fighting.

"Are you homeless because of your problems? Or have problems because you're homeless?"

"You married?"

"No."

"Are you like this because you ain't married? Or not married because you like this?"

"Like what?"

"Look at yourself," Chance says. "You a driven woman, too focused on work."

"That's the Puritan work ethic," I say. "This is where I've been trying to get my whole life."

"That's your problem right there."

"What kind of job are you looking for?"

"Parking cars."

Valet parkers are to Houston what taxi drivers are to New York. People valet-park at restaurants, hotel business meetings, the hairdresser, even the laundromat. I'm the only person in Houston who can't bring myself to hand over my car to someone I never saw before. "If people do it with Jaguars and Mercedes," Web used to say when I dated him, "why can't you?" Gabriel loves me whether I valet-park or not.

"Parking cars?" I say.

"Well, I went to truck-driving school, and I didn't get to graduate, but soon as I get myself together I'm going back," he says. "That's part of my goal."

"How are you getting yourself together?"

"My motivation is mostly in myself. I pretty much have my own ego. I'm in a situation now where I'm telling me, deep down inside, I know what I want to do, I know what I want to be."

"What do you want to be?"

"I know I can't be a singer, but I can sing, but what I really want to be?" He looks me in the eye. "I could be a nice dresser, live in a middle-class neighborhood, bring my kids up the *right* way. And just go out to restaurants with my wife, my lady-friend, just do things that married couples should do. That's my dream, that's my goal."

He wants what I want, what Gabriel wants.

My cellular phone rings. "You all right?" Gabriel says. "I suddenly got concerned about you."

"I'm downtown," I say, "interviewing a member of the homeless community."

"Page me if you need me to come get you."

"You can't leave the E.R."

"I'd send an ambulance."

After Gabriel hangs up, I tell Chance about my outreach project to bring the library to the homeless.

"Your problem," he says, "is you out of the loop, home-lesswise."

"Can you help me?"

He grins. "Stick with me. I know all kind of homeless, all over this city. The only thing I don't know nothing about is that Satan crap. If you go down this way, on Main Street, they got Satan's name written on this side, they got a skeleton here, bones, what do you call, the skinheads. There's a lot of that weird crap going on. But to me, I met some crazy peo-ple. I don't care if you homeless or not, you like me or you don't like me. A conversation's a conversation. You can be wild or a horse can be wild, you can ride it and break it, sooner or later you have his respect. I'm going to some places, then I'm coming back home, then I'm going to buy a brand-new car, what have you. I'm just going to live, that's it."

At least he's not going to Aruba. I'm dizzy from his ver-sion of a conversation, layer upon layer of problems. Can he sort out what was out of his control from what he could have made turn out better? The cause and effect is all out of whack.

"Are you leveling with me, Chance?"

"You ain't ready to hear the truth."

"Try me."

He draws himself together, fixes me in his bloodshot stare. "The human heart is broke."

"You're trying to heal your broken heart?"

"I *am* the broken heart," he says.

3

Visitation

Gabriel's ex-wife, Felicity, lives in an affluent part of Houston called Memorial, in a palatial new house with a walled garden. Gabriel spent his trust fund on it to make her happy, and as soon as the landscape architect drove away in a caravan with the interior designer, the painters, and the wallpaper people, she filed for divorce.

"Was Memorial named for a cemetery?" I ask.

"Became that for me," Gabriel says.

Gabriel is one of those men who couldn't imagine he'd get divorced, but Felicity was one of those little girls who were raised to get the house. "She'll get the house," I say whenever we see a little girl throwing a fit in Neiman Marcus.

Felicity has the unfortunate habit of twisting the rules for Gabriel's visitation with his two-year-old son for her convenience but never returning the favor. "If you want to see Gabe this weekend," she tells Gabriel over the phone, "you'll have to pick him up in San Antonio Saturday instead of at my house." I hear her; her breathy, little-girl voice is like a dagger dripping with honey.

"This is my weekend. The divorce decree says I pick him up at your house."

"I'm taking him to the Alamo," she says. "You'd deprive him of that?"

He sighs. "Okay, Felicity."

"Don't bring him back Sunday evening at six because I won't be back from San Antonio until ten."

"I have other plans Sunday evening," he says, and looks at me.

"I won't be back before ten."

"Get a babysitter."

"No," she says, and hangs up.

"You're not going to let her get away with it?" I say. "You could take her to court for not abiding by the divorce decree."

"She'd love to go back to court. She's got a litigious personality."

"She should go to law school."

"She does."

Gabriel will do anything to get his visitation because he has the terminal guilties. We drive three hours on Saturday morning to pick up Gabe at the Alamo. We talk across Gabe's empty car seat, between us in the front of the pickup. Actually, it's just me having our conversation; Gabriel doesn't say a thing. A lot of men are like that, but it's worse in Gabriel because he has more feelings not to express. The taciturnity hasn't been bred out of the cowboy in him; he just has more to think about now than cows.

"Have you ever been to Aruba?" I say, to take his mind off his problems with Felicity. I don't need Web to take me to Aruba. Maybe Gabriel and I will go if we ever have a honeymoon.

"I took Felicity there when we were trying to avoid a divorce," he says. "I'll never go to Aruba again."

At the Alamo, Gabriel climbs out of the pickup to lift Gabe from Felicity's gold Infiniti. Gabe loves Gabriel's black and white truck, but did Felicity teach him to call it the Cowmobile?

Felicity's a bottle blonde with straight-from-the-hairdresser Junior League hair. She's a bit younger than I, but, I'm pleased to see, many pounds fatter.

Gabriel introduces us but she refuses to acknowledge me. She leans across me to take off Gabe's shoes, then puts them in her purse.

"What's with Gabe's shoes?" I ask Gabriel as we drive away. "Is she afraid you'll keep them and send him back barefoot?"

He doesn't answer. Felicity acts crazy but Gabriel won't even spell it; he doesn't want Gabe to feel pulled between his parents. I know all this because Gabriel and I have been over it a hundred times. Felicity, on the other hand, wants to make Gabriel look like Satan to Gabe, so she scolds Gabriel in front of Gabe every chance she gets.

Gabe looks exactly like Gabriel—high forehead, blond hair, patrician nose—but with smooth, baby skin instead of Gabriel's rough and hairy. His forthright little chin must be a miniature version of the one Gabriel has under his beard. I worry that one of those little girls raised to get the house is going to get him in her clutches.

'Hello, Gabe," I say.

He doesn't answer, just puts his thumb in his mouth.

"Colleen lives with us now," Gabriel tells him.

Children usually love me; transfixed and happy, they stare as if they can see something about me I can't see myself. Gabe, on the other hand, takes sober measure with his wide blue eyes. He looks permanently surprised, as if he got off on the wrong planet.

"He's been through a lot for a little kid," Gabriel says. "Think he looks dazed?"

I do, but I don't want to make Gabriel feel more guilty than he does already. "He's an old soul," I say. "He wasn't expecting still another reincarnation." He wasn't expecting an extra mother-figure either, but it seems unwise to point this out.

"This'll be your last one," Gabriel says to Gabe, and hugs him. "Doesn't get any worse than this."

I'm wondering what to make of this when Gabe starts to cry for his shoes. We stop and buy him a pair of little blue jogging shoes, but he doesn't want to wear them; he wants to throw them on the floor of the truck and have me pick them up.

"He's his mother's child," I say.

Gabriel's eyes plead with me. Gabe has me over a barrel, Felicity has Gabriel over a barrel, and Gabriel and I are about to roll over Niagara Falls.

As soon as we get home, Gabe hands me his briefcase with his wet training pants inside. Felicity has given him some potty-training issues, but his Montessori school has taught him to carry dry pants everywhere.

"Thank you, Gabe," I say. I take it for the gesture of trust it is. I fall in love with him for the courage it must take to hand his wet pants not only to his mother, his father, and his teacher, but also this strange woman his father seems to like a lot.

"If he has an accident at school, they hand him a little mop so he can clean it up himself with a modicum of dignity," Gabriel says.

"I'd hate to see him grow up like me with an exaggerated sense of responsibility, " I say.

"He's learning to take responsibility for himself, where

you learned to take responsibility for other people."

"Everyone says the homeless refuse to take responsibility for themselves, but maybe they tried to take responsibility for people so awful they gave up on the notion of responsibility altogether," I say.

"More likely no one took responsibility for them as kids," he says, "so they grew into adults incapable of taking responsibility for themselves."

I throw the wet pants into the washing machine.

Gabriel and Gabe go outside to play in the prickly pear. I watch them from the balcony. They collect rocks in a pail, chase lizards, catch bugs. Gabriel looks up at me and waves. I wave back. They've been together longer than Gabriel and I. They have rituals I'm not part of. I make dinner—pasta puttanesca, a salad of baby field greens with julienned jicama and sun-dried tomatoes. It's not clear to me what role Gabe will play in my audition with Gabriel, but dinner seems a good place to start. When they come back in, the three of us sit on the balcony to watch the sunset.

Gabe won't eat the stuffed mushroom caps I baked as hors d'oeuvres. Gabriel gives him a piece of beef jerky instead. "He loves beef jerky," he says.

The sky reddens over the blackening earth. Even in the city, the Texas sunset overwhelms me because there's so much of it. Small dark birds fly low across the condo complex, singing, catching supper. The sun goes down behind the Houston skyline. The Galleria and the Transco Tower sink back into the night.

"Again," Gabe says to me.

"I beg your pardon?"

"I want to see it again!"

"The sunset?"

"Yes!" He gives up on me and looks at Gabriel, sure his father can make it happen all over right now.

"Not until tomorrow night, Gabe," Gabriel says. He picks him up and puts him into his chair for dinner. Gabriel made Gabe an elevated chair, out of the seat pulled from one of the ranch's tractors.

Gabe sits there as if he's two going on forty, until he plunges into his dinner. Felicity has given him some eating issues as well. Gabriel tries matter-of-factly to wipe up Gabe's spills, but he looks disconcerted, to say the least. Even with his camping bowls and spoons, Gabriel himself has table manners worthy of a ten-course dinner on state china.

"Next time he comes we'll have neater food," I say.

"Neatness doesn't always count," Gabriel says.

It turns out the only part of the salad Gabe will eat is the jicama. He picks it out with his pudgy fingers. "No 'matoes," he says.

"You liked the tomatoes in the spaghetti sauce, apparently," I say, but I see the futility in discussing this.

Felicity calls several times during dinner to talk to Gabe. He listens, his little face impassive.

"Is she asking him whether we're abusing him?" I ask Gabriel.

"I try not to let it get to me."

"It's worse than telemarketing."

"She'll escalate if she knows that," he says. He sponges Gabe's food off the phone still one more time.

"Would you like to send your mother a postcard?" I say to Gabe.

By the time dinner is over, we all look as if we've been fingerpainting, puttanesca sauce on our faces, up our arms, in our hair. Noodles hang from the chairs; jicama litters the room like confetti. I vacuum before we track arugula all over the apartment. Gabe gets his toy vacuum cleaner and cleans up beside me.

"He believes in equality between the sexes," I say.

"He's trying to be good," Gabriel says. He carries his dinner plate to the kitchen.

Gabe trudges along behind him, carries his plate to the kitchen.

"Kids this good grow up to be ax-murderers," I say.

Gabriel whisks Gabe off to the Jacuzzi, the next best thing to putting him entirely into the washing machine.

"You look like a new man," I say to Gabe when he comes back in his Superman pajamas with a tiny red cape.

Gabriel tells Gabe a bedtime story he makes up, about brave boys who catch enormous lizards, and heroic men who re-create sunsets on demand. The tightness of their bond is beginning to hurt.

"Why don't you put a girl in that story?" I say to Gabriel.

Gabriel makes up a character named Amber in a pink dress and ruffled socks who goes outside to smell the flowers after helping her mother bake cookies.

"Amber's a militant feminist," I say. "She wouldn't be caught dead baking cookies in pink ruffled socks."

The next big hurdle we face is sleeping arrangements. "Where does Gabe usually sleep?" I ask.

"In his own sleeping bag next to the futon."

"On the floor?"

"If he falls out of bed, he doesn't have anyplace to fall."

"I'll sleep in your study," I say.

"Gabe'll start sleeping in the study."

"He won't like that."

"We all have to make some adjustments here," he says to Gabe, man to man.

I'm relieved to see Gabe gets to nestle down in the study with his blanket, his thumb, and his bunny. The Montessori people don't have to know. Even the soft furry bunny looks like Gabriel and Gabe, blond with big blue button eyes.

"My bunny," Gabe says to me, introducing us.

"Yes!" I hug the bunny.

"Mine!" Gabe says, and grabs it back as if to say you can sleep with my father, but you can't sleep with my bunny.

Gabriel tells Gabe one more story while I fix us a night-cap of blackberry tea. Gabriel could probably use a Lone Star longneck, but he won't have one with Gabe here. Southern parents never drink in front of their children, while Yankee parents insist theirs drink with them.

Finally Gabriel tiptoes out of Gabe's room, leaving on the dinosaur nightlight. He sinks into his chair, takes a sip of tea. "This is really weird."

"You're telling me," I say.

"This is the sort of thing I'd think immoral if someone told me about it. In the situation myself, I can see everyone's side of it."

"A lot of things in life are like that."

We read instead of talk, so we won't wake up Gabe. Gabriel reads the Bible in a paroxysm of guilt. I can't bring myself to go that far, so I read an old copy of *Reader's Digest* to try to assimilate into normal white-bread America.

I lie awake all night next to Gabriel sleeping, and listen for the slightest whimper from Gabe's room. If he wakes up, I'll have no choice but to go immediately to the Motel 6 down the street.

•

"We made it," I say to Gabriel when Sunday morning finally comes. Baby birds in the trees outside cheep wildly for their breakfasts. I'm so exhausted I can hardly lean up on one elbow.

"Made what?" Gabriel says.

"What?" Gabe says, nestled into the soft edge of the futon. Gabriel has his arm around Gabe and Gabe has his little arm around his bunny.

"Never mind," I say. "What's Gabe like for breakfast?"

"Yogurt," Gabriel says.

"Kids don't like yogurt. What kind?"

"Plain, nonfat. Gabe is nutritionally aware."

Gabe must like yogurt, because a few minutes into breakfast we all look as if we've been fingerpainting again.

"We have to subscribe to some parenting magazines," I say to Gabriel. "This is too much to wing."

"You raised your younger brother while your mother was at work. You started when he was two and you were four."

"Maybe that's why I feel so inadequate."

We're going to the zoo today. Gabriel dresses Gabe in a terminally cute Sunday outfit—a navy blue suit with white shirt and red suspenders. Gabe has a full supply of clothes, equipment, and toys at Gabriel's, and another set of everything at his mother's.

"Head 'em up!" Gabriel says.

We walk down the stairs.

At the zoo, Gabriel carries Gabe on his shoulders. A double person, they weave through the pillars and hanging baskets of flowers outside the monkey house. The monkeys swing in their cage from tree to tree, wrap their rubbery arms around each other. Gabe wraps his arms around Gabriel's head, clings to his hair. He appropriates Gabriel to himself.

I traipse along behind them. Gabriel and Gabe in their

own world, I'm surrounded by other people and their children. The baboons make a terrible din. My father took my brother and me to the zoo, but we were too afraid of him to enjoy it. I'd hope my father wouldn't want a drink, but if he did, my brother and I waited outside the bar for him, locked in the car. Hours later, he'd drop us off at home. Our mother waited at the front window. "I was worried sick," she'd say.

At the elephants, a young elephant won't let a smaller one out of the pool. The baby grows more and more unhappy, until the mother elephant comes out to see what's the matter. The baby lumbers to his mother with a shriek, waving his trunk.

We go on to the lions and tigers, then the giraffes and the tropical birds. Gabe wants to ride the miniature train. The train travels through the park, past the cages, under the trees. Gabe and Gabriel sit together, and I sit behind them, squeezed into a child-sized seat next to a woman who reminds me of Felicity. She has green eyes like Felicity's— doll's eyes so well-defined with makeup and lashes they could stick open or shut.

There's no breeze; the warm, heavy air grows dark. Gabe babbles to Gabriel about Mommy. It's Gabe's job to break up my relationship with Gabriel and get his parents back together. They're still a family, on some fundamental level.

It starts to pour as we get off the train. Gabriel finds a clean Hefty bag, makes a hole for Gabe's head and puts it over him. Gabriel and I get soaked, but Gabe, at least, is dry. He races to a waterfall pouring from a roof spout, stands under it, ecstatic.

"Gabe!"I say. I scold him in spite of myself.

His eyes fill with hurt surprise. With Felicity's green and Gabriel's blue in his eyes, he has the sadness of both. A child's capacity for sadness isn't small; he is pure sadness.

"I'm sorry," I say. I kneel down to hug him, my own eyes full of tears. Do my eyes carry my mother's and my father's sorrow?

His eyes change color with forgiveness.

"I'm starting to care about him," I say to Gabriel. "When you feel how someone's feeling, that's the beginning of the end."

"No," Gabriel says. He takes both me and Gabe into his arms. "It's the beginning of the beginning."

4

Beginner Self-Defense

Gigi and I meet at the Women's Center for our first class in Beginner Self-Defense.

"Would you rather be in Aruba with Web or Houston with Gabriel?" she says, when I tell her how off balance Web's phone call threw me.

"In Aruba with Gabriel," I say.

She and I were inseparable at Our Lady of Perpetual Sorrows, a girls' high school in Boston. Between then and our move to Houston, she married and divorced a stuffed shirt named Henry. We used to visit every evening in the hallway between our apartments in the Lord's Motel. We strategized about men and our jobs, gossiped, scolded each other, cheered each other on. Best friends in our checkered past, we still are in our checkered present.

"Fantasize Aruba when you're having sex," she says. She's petite, but her chic black Euro-hair gives her a kind of feminist Napoleonic authority.

"Houston sex is okay," I say. "Except early in the morning before I'm ready to face my intimacy issues."

"If you get married," she says, "you'll be glad to get it when you can."

"Would marriage make my intimacy issues go away?"

"You need self-defense," she says, "to defend yourself against yourself."

Bubba Dooley, our self-defense instructor, looks like a pregnant Frankenstein straight out of Gabriel's army surplus catalog. Bursting with padding, his green and brown camouflage jumpsuit sticks out at the crotch. He bends over to lace up his combat boots, buckle on his black leather shinguards. His eyes glow like cinders through the holes of his padded helmet.

"Ninety percent of this is enthusiasm," Bubba says. "When you strike you got to explode!"

After I promised Vanessa I'd take self-defense to protect myself from the homeless, I talked Gigi into taking it with me. Gigi talked Barbara into it, Barbara talked Marcy into it, and Marcy talked Susan into it. That's what networking is all about.

"I wish we were taking Quilting or Conversational Spanish instead," I say. It's heartbreaking to take self-defense to protect myself from Chance's broken heart.

"Everyone in our generation takes lessons in something," Gigi says. "Media training, makeup lessons, executive leadership."

"We need a lot of improvement," I say.

"Lessons are what we do with our lives," she says.

Bubba lines us up. He shows each of us the part of the palm to strike with, how to stand, punch with our weight behind it. He corrects me as I slug him; my strikes are off-center, too timid, too slow. He holds onto my wrist to pull the punch from my shoulder. "See how fast you can do that?" he says, then moves on to the others.

"It's not that our lovemaking isn't good," I say to Gigi. "It's just not the way I thought it would be."

"What do you want?"

"That's what I'm trying to find out. Making love with Gabriel is too intense to think my way through."

I watch Gigi slug Bubba as if she's been doing it all her life. People who never had a problem with sex never understand the people who do.

"Do sensate focus exercises with Gabriel," she says after her turn.

"Gabriel doesn't *want* to do sensate focus exercises."

"Tell him he has to."

"I don't want to rock the bed."

"Every man has a tragic flaw," she says, after a pause. "But you need to ask yourself why you're willing to put up with that particular one."

"After being so compliant with Web, part of me has to admire someone like Gabriel who won't go along with someone else's program."

"You can admire the heck out of it," she says, "but how will you get what you want?"

"That's a problem. It's ironic that with Web I got what he wanted, and now with Gabriel I get what he wants."

"You might examine that for any discernible pattern," she says.

We watch Barbara punch Bubba. Barbara's an international loan officer who grew up bulldogging cattle on a ranch near Waco. She lives in the Lord's Motel like Gigi. Six feet tall, with wide birthing hips, she got pregnant by a welder who came to use the pay phone outside. The welder's out of the picture, but we're all crazy about her one-year-old, Dusty.

"Barbara figured out what she wanted," I say, "then she found the man for the job."

We widen our stances, lunge forward. We practice our punches on the air.

"I found a new man on the information superhighway," Gigi says.

"What was he driving?" I say.

"It was love at first byte," she says. "Malcolm and I are aheady having Internet."

"What happened to Jack?" Gigi's former boyfriend works for Cow Patty Software just as she does, but the main thing they had in common was their sex life.

"Jack and I are still disinfecting computers," she says. "But Malcolm has a big hard disk."

"How do you know Malcolm isn't having Internet with everybody?"

"Malcolm's very virtual."

Gigi and I sat through retreats together at Our Lady of Perpetual Sorrows. A priest was brought in to tell us the evils of sex, because the nuns were too refined. Gigi twisted her hanky from self-abuse and petting all the way up to the back seat of a car. My worst suspicions were confirmed when she came out of the confessional crying and had to spend study hall in chapel doing penance. From then on, Gigi could do no right. Her uniform was too tight, her grades fell, she was rumored to have started smoking. Poor Gigi.

"Poor Jack," I say.

"Not really," she says. "It turns out Jack's been fucking Houston."

"All of it?"

"The problem with the world today," she says, "is not homelessness or crime. It's men like Jack who drop their shorts for anyone."

"Like Web," I say. "Wouldn't you think with all his girl-friends he'd leave me alone?"

Bubba teaches us to kick, our target the triangle of armor over his groin. "Eighty-nine percent will stop at a convincing 'Stay back!'" he says. "It's the other eleven percent you got to worry about."

"Stay back!" I shout as he strides toward me.

"Nyuck, nyuck," he says, still coming.

I set my stance, keep my eye on the target, deliver my kick. "That's only a C-plus," he says. "You kick too *nice*."

"How do I drop the defenses I learned with Web to make really good love with Gabriel?" I ask Gigi when Bubba moves on to Marcy.

"You're like one of those people who spend all their time and money trying to get on the info superhighway, then don't know what to do when they get there."

"I sort of get what I want. I just have to work too hard to get it."

"You have all your multimedia hardware properly installed but you're missing the right software drivers."

"What do the drivers do?"

"Tell the computer how to communicate with the peripherals," she says. "Like you need to learn with Gabriel."

"It's a steep learning curve," I say.

Marcy looks straight out of step aerobics in her tights and leotard, but her kick sends Bubba staggering backwards. "What if we really hurt someone?" she asks.

"That's the point," Bubba says. "The mugger should've thought of that; it's what he gets for attacking you girls. Some of these techniques could kill a mugger, like stomping on his head when he's down."

We flinch.

"I don't have that fear of hurting someone who attacks me *in* me, on account of I'm a man," he goes on. "The way you girls have been brought up, to be nurturing and stuff like that, it's going to be harder for you. All I'm asking, is you got to be *total animals* for ten or fifteen seconds. Beats the heck out of what you get if you don't."

Bubba attacks us from behind, shows us how to kick him in the shins, stomp on his feet, spin around, knee him in the head.

"I feel like a one-legged man in a kickin' contest," Barbara says. Her back toward Bubba, she waits to be attacked.

"You're going to be afraid," Bubba says. He takes off his shinguards to readjust the buckles. "You got to develop the personality where it goes right through you. The mugger's good at being scary; he's done this a lot. *You* got to be good at defending yourself, where you got the confidence."

We know something's wrong when we don't hear the *thwack* of Barbara's shoe against the hard buckles. Bubba has forgotten to put his shinguards back on. He limps away without a word.

Barbara feels awful. We change the subject to bank loans, to cheer her up and give Bubba a chance to recover.

"Tell us again how you got promoted during the Houston banking crisis," Marcy says to Barbara.

"Not to get fired was to get promoted," she says.

His shinguards back on, Bubba stands behind me. His feet paw the floor; he growls and makes other threatening noises. My heart pounds; I do my best to prepare myself. He throws his arms around me, pins mine to my sides. Kicking and stomping, I feel pathetic, almost cute. I fight to break his grasp, free my arms for elbow jabs to his sides. I spin around. He offers his helmeted head to meet my knee coming up.

"Tell me more about you and Gabriel," Gigi says after class.

"I can't. Not only will you tell everyone, you'll exaggerate."

"I never betray confidences."

"No, you just tell everyone who put what where."

"He did?" she says. "Where did he put it? What did he put?"

5

The Christening

I fly the next weekend to Boston, for my niece Chelsea's christening. I'm her godmother.

Gabriel wanted to come but I wouldn't let him. "Let me prepare them," I said. In my family I'm on the maiden-aunt track. Gabriel would have insisted, but Felicity gave him Gabe this weekend so she could go to the Virgin Islands. If Gabriel and I married but never had a child, would he stay more married to Felicity than to me?

My brother Doug stares at me in my red cowboy boots, jeans, fringed shirt, rodeo-style hat. I'm perpetrating the Texas stereotype on the East Coast. Doug can look Ivy League in his pajamas—that's what good schools do for you. Andover, Amherst, Harvard Business School. He was the most brilliant boy in the project when we were growing up. The worst moment of Doug's life was when Tony Palomi threw his slide rule down the sewer.

"How are things going with Web?" Pamela, Doug's wife, asks.

Polished and sleek, Pamela did everything right and it worked. I did everything right at first, but it didn't work, then I did everything wrong and that didn't either.

"Actually, I'm living with someone else."

Pamela's lips twitch as if she'd purse them but doesn't want to wrinkle. She saw that beneath his prep-school exterior, Web was dysfunctional enough to fit in. "Don't lose your advantage before marriage," she says. "We want you to be happy."

"I *am* happy."

"No you're not."

"I worry a lot, but that's not the same as being unhappy."

"Anyway, get married soon," Pamela says. "At your age it could take a long time to get pregnant." She leads us on tiptoe into the nursery.

Chelsea curls sound-asleep in her crib, a halo around her downy head. The three of us shine down on her like suns. What is it that makes newborn babies look so heavy, like little flannel sacks of flour? Not floating anymore, cast up on a beach somewhere, she's too astonished at her own small mass to take responsibility for it. Gravity is all she needs to know.

Pamela picks her up and leads us into the living room. Doug opens the liquor cabinet for the christening party; Pamela breast-feeds Chelsea. I'm standing in the cold spot in a warm ocean. They live a life that won't let me in; I'm locked out of the heavenly suburbs, where everything is decorated out of existence. It's an Add-a-Pearl necklace sort of life. "I just want to do things that married couples should do," Chance said. "That's my dream, that's my goal."

"Have you always been this happy?" I ask Pamela.

Pamela was a daddy's girl—an object of love I can't even imagine. She has all this stuff she loves. When she wants more, she gets it and loves that too; she grows progressively more contented, more shiny in her expensive cosmetics.

People like me do all the worrying for people like Pamela.

"When I was Miss Teenage Massachusetts," she says, "you were already an existentialist."

Sober, solid, dependable, Doug takes glasses out of the cabinet behind the bar.

"Congratulations," I say to him. "You must be thrilled about Chelsea."

He shakes his head of sandy Irish hair. "I'll be happier when Dad has come and gone," he says.

We've squeezed our father out of Christmas and Thanksgiving but we haven't figured out how to squeeze him out of baptisms or funerals. At Christmas, he played Santa drunk, breaking the toys moments after assembling them. Dougie cried in his crib. Thanksgivings, while families talked and laughed around their tables, our father heard the shriek of the hunted bird. He jumped up when rage took hold of him. He seized things, not knowing what he was seizing. Afterwards, with the smell of apples warming on the trees, the sky bright blue above the orange and yellow leaves, he opened the bulkhead and went down into the cellar to brood among his nails and tools.

I talked Doug and Pamela into inviting him to Chelsea's christening, making myself suspect. "How's it look?" my father asked when he called me out of the blue. "Not so good," I said. "If they don't let me see the kid now," he said, "they never will."

"Okay, so none of us would pick him to be our best friend," I say to Doug, "but what's so terrible about him now that he doesn't drink?"

"He's manipulative," Doug says. "He acts as if all he wants is to see his grandchild before he dies."

"That's the only way he knows to get anything he wants," I say. "It's pathetic, but he's desperate."

"I hate pathetic people," Doug says.

"I do too." I'm like a defense attorney who doesn't believe in her client. A breeze as full as a sigh lifts the lower branches of the tree outside the window. My father sighs like that. "If you knew what his childhood was like, it would curdle your blood," I go on. "He drank to find unity between himself and his mother because his mothering was horribly disturbed at an early oral level of development." Pamela is still nursing Chelsea; I cup my hand over the soft spot in the baby's head to protect her from these crazy ideas.

"Some people are just rotten," Doug says. "It's not that anything made them that way, they just are. They don't have any character."

"He's trying to make amends." I can't understand why I've taken up my father's cause except that he and I are two kinds of scapegoats. If I help my father, will the gods of relationship look kindly on me and let me have a life with Gabriel?

"We don't want any amends he'd make," Doug says.

Doug doesn't need to forgive, he already has a wife and a baby and a house in the suburbs. I'm here, single, while the man I love is with the child he had with somebody else.

"He has no manners," Pamela says. "He interrupts; he jiggles."

"He's afraid of us," I say. "When he senses I accept him, he calms down and says more interesting things."

"I don't trust him as far as I can throw him," Doug says.

"Trust?" I say, as Pamela carefully hands Chelsea to me. Chelsea is too small to arrange herself in my arms; I arrange her until her small weight settles. When Doug and I were children, we took floating lessons at Swampy Pit. A dead horse was said to be buried there; I couldn't put my head into the water. Our floating teacher gestured with hands as soft as petals. "Trust your brother," she said. My head in Doug's cupped hands, I lay down in the water. The skirt of my bathing suit blossomed like a flower.

The doorbell chimes. My mother sails in, billowing in flowered silk, followed by her brother Robert and his companion Sidney. Robert and Sidney are defrocked priests who met in the seminary, and now they share a hyphenated last name. They're *my* godparents, dressed today in navy pinstripes and red ties. With Chelsea in my arms, I suddenly feel as if I'm at the University Club at cocktail hour with a baby.

"Hello dear, hello dear, hello dear," my mother says to me, Doug, and Pamela in turn. Protected and reassured, my mother takes on a more festive personality when she's with Robert and Sidney. She should have married someone debonair like Sidney, but Robert got him.

Sidney eyes my boots and jeans. "Loretta Lynn!"

"Anyone like a drink?" Doug says. He makes three martinis with the vermouth just waved over them for my mother and Robert and Sidney.

"How's Texas?" Sidney asks me.

"Anarchic," I say. "Especially on the freeways."

"That's enough out of you, Bernadette Devlin," Robert says. With Robert and Sidney, I'm Loretta Lynn one minute, Bernadette Devlin the next—I never have to take myself seriously with them. They have high-paying jobs with the I.R.S. That's the most I've been able to find out about what they do. They never discuss their jobs with me because I might let some national secret slip in a singles' bar and the whole American government would collapse. They secretly believe themselves corrupt, but they're the Fathers Know Best of their set.

Robert balances his martini on his kneecap while Sidney lays out a long line of vitamins for him on the coffee table:

gigantic vitamin E capsules gelatinous with golden nectar; red, blue, green buttons in different sizes. Sidney is solicitous of Robert, the way I am of Gabriel. Robert washes down a fistful of pills with his martini.

"Colleen," Pamela says, "help me get Chelsea into her christening dress."

I hop up, dutiful godmother that I am. Robert must never abdicate as patriarch. On the other hand, everyone is afraid my father will never die, and I'm terrified he'll linger on, ancient and decrepit, with only me to take care of him. I'll go from unripe middle-age to caring for a homeless father with no wifehood or motherhood in between.

I help Pamela guide Chelsea's tiny hands through the sleeves of her long white dress.

Chelsea wails.

I pick her up. "Hang in there, kiddo."

She scrunches up her face when Pamela puts on her white bonnet.

After I dress for the christening, we all squeeze into Doug and Pamela's Volvo. I'm wondering where my father is, after all my trouble to wangle an invitation for him, when he drives up in a small, battered rental car.

"You ride with him," Doug says to me.

My father grins when I climb in. He's the Water Grandfather, the shifter of shapes who lives in the river, in the woods outside the village. Dangerous, seductive, impish, he dances on moonlit nights with drowned women he marries. I'm his reluctant daughter, pale and melancholy, singing in the trees. He's Pan, growing old. I'm afraid to love him, afraid not to, so I subject myself to his disguises. But he's out of his water element, and the villagers want revenge. I'm afraid of what will happen if I don't protect him.

"Follow Doug, Dad," I say, as Doug's Volvo starts down

the driveway, between the tall elms and maples.

His mouth turns down again, the creases worn in all the way to his jawbone, a sad rainbow. He goes through his entire repertoire of compulsive tics—puts his foot on the accelerator then brakes suddenly, throws his hands from the steering wheel to smooth remembered hair from his bald head, clears his throat with a loud "Haaaaaarrumph!" Cars honk on both sides of us as he swerves first to the right lane, then back to the left. He grabs the turn signal but turns on the windshield wipers instead, adjusts his thick glasses, then bounces desperately to settle back in his seat.

I flop from side to side even in my seatbelt; it's like riding in a boat. My father's symphony of nervous gestures makes me anxious the way Stravinsky does. *Objects in mirror are closer than they appear* is stencilled on the sideview mirror.

"I borrowed a disposable camera," he says.

"Don't take any photos unless they invite you to," I say.

He does it to give himself something to do while everyone is excluding him from their conversations, and also to prove to himself later he was there. He's creating a family history for himself. "Everyone will be glad to see the pictures twenty years from now," he says.

"Not if all they remember is how uncomfortable they felt while you were taking them," I say. He showed up at my high school prom with a movie camera and floodlights.

I keep my eyes glued to Doug's Volvo up ahead. Doug's whole life is an effort to do everything excessively right to compensate for Dad's screw-ups.

My father stops to wait for a green light to turn yellow, then red. "I know a shortcut," he says, as Doug's car fades out of sight.

"We don't even know where the church is!"

"Don't get excited, honey."

He drives on aimlessly until I pound the car door with my fist. "I'm the godmother! " I say. "Damn it, you're *trying* to get us lost—you *want* to screw it up!" I jump out of my father's rental car and run down the road in my dress and high heels. Doug's car is waiting around the corner.

"We could see he wasn't paying any attention," my mother says when I squeeze in next to her.

I have the kind of despair from running a race through exhaustion and into the finish where although you want to stop you have to run forever. At the church, Pamela places Chelsea in my arms. I walk to the altar with Chelsea's godfather, whom I haven't even met.

Chelsea sleeps through her christening, stirs only when the priest pours the baptismal water on her forehead.

"Wasn't Chelsea good?" Pamela says, as everyone gathers around us after the ceremony.

My father stands by himself at the back of the church, dangling my purse the way men do.

No one makes me ride back with him for the christening party.

Doug pops the corks from the bottles of champagne. I help Pamela spread the beautiful little sandwiches and hors d'oeuvres on the dining room table. Pamela takes a cup of coffee to my father.

"Why's he just standing there like that?" Doug says.

"He's waiting for someone to invite him to take pictures," I say.

"Not while we're eating," Doug says.

Neighbors and friends arrive with presents for Chelsea faster than Pamela can open them—music boxes, silver cups and spoons. My mother helps Pamela unwrap pink boxes of baby clothes. Chelsea wears the tiny Add-a-Pearl necklace I gave her. Robert and Sidney present Doug with Chelsea's first portfolio of stocks and bonds.

The party chatter is sprinkled with the clink of champagne flutes. Everyone laughs and talks, except my father. My mother acts as if he's someone to whom she has never been introduced and has no wish to be. Robert and Sidney are masters at party behavior; they gave him the receiving-line handshake that sends the recipient down the line before he knows what hit him. He can't afford the most commonplace social risks. "Don't talk anyone's ear off," I'd told him, and now he's afraid to open his mouth.

He walks to the window. He gazes out, examines the weather, a warm swirl of color outside as vivid as the one inside. But he doesn't see it. What's more terrifying than feeling completely alone at a party? Being ignored is worse than being despised. The chatter of the crowd surrounds you like a moat. You hear disembodied voices. Your own voice sinks so deeply into the knot in your throat that no one hears you even if you speak. You're invisible; you're dead.

He puts his finlike hands into the pockets of his old tweed sportcoat and turns halfway around, as if he's looking for something. He's shaped like a top, narrow-shouldered, his belly ballooning out, his short legs converging in his flat feet. He wobbles like a top winding down. His front teeth clamp down on his lower lip, an old habit from when he used to smoke a pipe. Now he has no pipe, no pouch of tobacco in his pockets. When he lifts his pockets with his hands still in them, his sportcoat blooms like a tent. He can't collect himself; his thought are too diffuse.

I walk through the crowd to my father. The guests feel the shift in the ranks as they pour drinks, reach for sandwiches, pass around the baby. No one looks in our direction but Doug, who gives me a grateful look. Everything is where it's supposed to be, but nothing really works right. My father and I are off to one side of the room, in our own lucid suburb of confusion. Has he developed his loneliness like a talent?

A drunk man shouldn't have unsupervised visitation with children, the courts said. My mother explained it to me.

No one offers to let my father hold Chelsea. I retrieve her from my mother and bring her back. He's afraid to ask to hold her, so I hand her to him carefully. I wave to Doug and Pamela across the room.

Chelsea looks up at her grandfather and screams.

Pamela rushes over. "She's just tired." She takes her off to the nursery.

Now that the guest of honor has left the party, the other guests begin to leave.

My father is more conspicuous when the living room has emptied out except for family. He's not family anymore. "I'm the one who made the baby cry," he says. Misshapen and out of place, he gets up to leave.

"Thank you for coming," Pamela says to him. She learned that at Smith.

Doug forces himself to shake Dad's hand; Robert and Sidney give him manly nods.

"Goodbye, Harry," my mother murmurs.

"Did you hear that?" my father says as I walk him out to his car. "That's the first time in twenty years your mother has called me by my name."

"I'm sorry you were so uncomfortable, Dad."

"I was just waiting for someone to suggest I take some pictures." He drives away.

Doug hands out another round of drinks for the post-party quarterbacking. "Was that enough amends for you?" he says to me.

"What is he talking about?" my mother asks me.

"Colleen had us invite Dad to Chelsea's christening so he could make amends," Doug says.

"How can he make amends after what he's done?" my mother says.

"Nevertheless, it was kind of you to say goodbye to him personally," I tell her.

"Goodbye is something I'll always be happy to tell him," she says. "But I don't understand why you're on this kick to forgive your father." She's afraid for us, the drowned girls the Water Grandfather marries.

"What's this about your moving in with someone?" Robert says.

Pamela must have discussed it with Doug, who told my mother, who told Robert. It's Robert's job to deal with me, since my judgment in everything is suspect to them for seeming to side with my father.

"Is this decisive?" my mother says.

The room falls still. My father, the one person who'd take my side whether I said yes or no, has gone. It's not that I take his side, it's just that I hate to see him standing on his side so alone.

"I love Gabriel," I say. "He's wonderful."

They look collectively dubious. Before I have a chance to say more, the cab comes to take me back to the airport.

On my flight back to Houston, I pull the phone handset from my seat's armrest and call Gigi. "Dr. Ruth said she could've helped Princess Diana and Prince Charles avoid a breakup," I say.

"Are you telling me you're going to break up with Gabriel over sex?"

"Dr. Ruth said she'd do it for free."

"I'll do yours for free."

"My mind and body are breaking up over Gabriel," I say. 'My body is like Camilla Parker-Bowles, but my mind is Princess Di."

"You don't know Prince Charles."

"Princess Di had to take the whole royal family to bed with her," I say. "Just like I can't really get away from mine."

"How does Gabriel feel about this?"

"He helps my body drag my mind along kicking and screaming."

"You're a sexual eccentric," she says.

The two passengers on either side of my middle seat lean in to eavesdrop better. One's a preppy pretty-boy who reminds me of Web. The other reminds me of my mother.

"I can't take up any more air time about it," I tell Gigi.

"We'll talk more later," she says.

Gabriel greets me at the door, draws me into his arms. He buries his face in the softness of my hair. "I missed you," he says, his breath hot and quick.

He begins a slow, careful seduction, but my lips taste the spice of his skin. Orange, cumin, cayenne, it steams with his musky love.

"I missed you too—" I say, then gasp when his kiss shoots through me. Icy hot, his desire lights me up from within.

His hand flips between us, unzipping, unbuckling. He brushes me, cupping and palming.

Our clothes in a trail from the door, we half-lead, half-follow each other. Aching with love, I fall to the sofa in the living room. The black leather is cool beneath me. He sinks, so warm, to my side. His sex is both fruit and flower, pendulous in its leaves. He creates me all over with his touch, soft and strong where I am smooth and wet. I lose myself in the textures of his body—his hair rough as crushed Indian paintbrush, tawny skin velvet with rippling muscle. I bask in the scent of him, earthy as ranch land, pungent as Gulf of Mexico brine.

We make love all night long. He plays me like a Texas fiddle, coaxes music from me I've never heard before. Waltz, blues, jazz notes twanging, I fall in love with him over and over again. We fall asleep in each other's arms, deep in the blue Texas dawn.

6

The Zulu Master

At least I've learned to activate the automatic gate of the God's Country Club parking lot by driving my bug back and forth over the sensor. I feel as if I'm ironing the driveway.

My library outreach study includes proposed methods for teaching the homeless to read. I stop at the library to find some materials but nothing seems relevant.

"We can't afford to overwhelm them with printed pages of gibberish about the middle class," I tell Vanessa in her mahogany-panelled office.

"How else do you propose to bring them into the mainstream?" she says. She grew up in a housing project as I did, then went to Vassar on a scholarship. Her clothes are elegantly tailored, her jewelry real. Her black skin is flawless.

I'm dying to ask her how she blends her eye shadow so perfectly, but I doubt she'd take mentoring that far. "We have to acknowledge the validity of their own experience first," I say.

"Fine," she says. "Take everything we have on an appropriate reading level written from the homeless point of view."

"I'll have them create their own materials," I say. "It's an approved method."

Vanessa's secretary, Lucille, interrupts us to usher a tiny, brittle lady into the office.

"Mrs. Gotraux," Vanessa says, "this is Colleen Sweeney, who's doing a study of library outreach to the homeless with a literacy component."

Mrs. Gotraux wears a mink stole, mustard-colored suit, felt hat, brown alligator shoes and purse. People this thin wear mink even in Houston's heat because they don't have much of a lipid layer. She wears huge rings on all ten fingers, even her thumbs. These accoutrements notwithstanding, she's so small I worry she'll fall into the crack between the sofa cushions and we'll never get her out.

"Idn't that lovely?" Mrs. Gotraux says. "But as children they must have learned to read in school."

"Unfortunately, some of them didn't," I say.

"Those must have been black children."

"Some of them are white."

"Then they didn't learn because they can't understand the black teachers they have nowadays," she says.

Vanessa's composure remains magisterially intact. "Mrs. Gotraux is interested in funding a unique library project," she says evenly to me.

"Taking library materials to the homeless is very unique," I say.

"I have never approved of the homeless hangin' out in public libraries," Mrs. Gotraux says.

"They won't come into the library if we go to them," Vanessa says to her. "Now will they?"

"We're missing the point here," I say.

"Would you be so kind as to ask my secretary to bring in the tea?" Vanessa says to me. She tosses her long black hair in a way Tina Turner would envy, then gives me her leave-before-you-screw-this-up look.

"So lovely to have met you," I say to Mrs. Gotraux as I stomp out.

I bump into Lucille standing just outside the mahogany door. She holds the silver tray and tea service. "Watch it," she says. "We spent your homeless budget on these petit fours."

"What were you waiting for?" I say.

"You to leave," Lucille says. "You don't get tea with the director unless you're associate director."

"*Until* I'm associate director," I say to scare Lucille a little.

Never happen," she says, and puts her shoulder to Vanessa's office door. She gives me a smile as appallingly sweet as the petit fours. Since she became Vanessa's secretary, Lucille has been going to smarm school.

Chance calls to say two teenage runaways will talk to me in return for lunch at a McDonald's in Montrose.

"Did you finish high school?" I ask Chance when I meet him outside.

He nods vaguely. "The ones that didn't finish school are the ones with the most negative attitude," he says. "That's how it goes."

"How would you get them to finish school?"

"That's a pretty hard one. Sometime or another, all the students have problems at home. The father can be on drugs if he's there, the mother can be on drugs, they can be an alcoholic. There's a lot of sex abuse goes on at home. This is what makes that average young person take life harder than one who had a real nice life. It's a shadow you forever carry with you."

I know about the shadow you carry with you. My father carries one and gave one to me. Whether I can return Gabriel's love depends on what I do with my shadow. With Web I believed if I couldn't be sexual and good, what the hell, I'd just be bad.

I slip Chance a twenty for his help, but feel as if I'm doing a drug deal.

"You married yet?"

"No," I say.

"You must not *want* to be married."

"It's not that simple."

"Then you don't *deserve* to be married," he says. "The married are different from you and me."

"Getting married is a basic human right."

"I got a dependence problem," he says, and shakes his head. "But you got a independence problem."

At a back booth in McDonald's, he introduces me to a bedraggled young couple, Reggie and Kathy. They look afraid they'll be thrown out any minute.

"I'm happy to meet you both," I say. I sit down with them.

"Button your shirt, man," Chance says to Reggie, then abandons the three of us to ourselves.

White, slight, about nineteen, Reggie buttons his tattered shirt over his hairless chest. He and Kathy look so hungry I suggest we order right away.

"We already know what we want," Reggie says. He orders Big Macs, fries, and Cokes for each of them.

"Where do you live, Reggie?" I say, putting my foot in my rapport.

"Nowhere."

"Where did you sleep last night?"

"I didn't."

"What did you do?"

"Partied."

"We all need a little recreation," I say, after a moment. "What sort?"

"Drugs."

My heart goes out to them in their limp, dirty clothes. "Where do you get the money to buy drugs?" I say.

"I zulu," he says. "I sell my wife to a trick for twenty dollars and I burn with it." He holds out his needle-tracked arm. "They call me the Zulu Master."

I turn to Kathy. "You get money for him?"

"People give it to me," she says.

"They just give it to you?"

"Hustlin'."

"Why?"

"I don't have nowhere else to go," she says. A once-pretty girl of about seventeen, her pallid skin is blotched. She clings to Reggie as if she wants me to talk with her only through him.

"Where do you do this?" I say to Reggie.

"On Westheimer, three in the afternoon, five in the morning, anytime."

"Would you like to learn to read and get a job?"

"I got no I.D. to get a job," he says. "But I can read a few words."

"Words are the building blocks of reading," I say. I sound ridiculous. "Sentences are made up of words, paragraphs are made up of sentences of words, books are made up of paragraphs of sentences of words, whole libraries are filled with books made up of paragraphs of sentences of words."

Kathy stares at Reggie to see if he's taking this in.

"Let's begin by reading the words you yourself said," I say, inspired by her almost imperceptible squeeze of his tracked arm. I print two of his declarative sentences and read them out loud: "'I zulu. I sell my wife to a trick for twenty dollars and I burn with it.' Is there anything you'd like to change?"

"No," Reggie says. He leans eagerly over his words. "That's what I said." He does his best to read them aloud, but stumbles over those with more than three letters.

I underline *zulu, wife,* and *burn,* then print each on a three-by-five card. "Let's begin with these," I say.

"He never had trouble before with four-letter words," Kathy says.

Reggie grins back, pokes her in the ribs.

"Kathy," I say, as I print the sentence, "'People give me money for hustling.'"

"They do?" she says.

"No," I say. "Those are *your* words. You can read them back to me—try."

"'People give me money for—*hustling,*'" she reads. "I couldn't read the last word but I guessed."

"Good," I say. "That's called 'context.' You figured out the word from the others in the sentence."

I print *hustling* on a three-by-five card for Kathy, shuffle all four cards, and quiz them both. "This is really wonderful," I say when they've got the words by sight.

They beam. We eat our lunch and play with the cards, like kids caught up in a game, oblivious to the noise in McDonald's. They stand in line to order dessert. I wish I could have brought them some of Vanessa's petit fours. We spend another hour experimenting with different techniques for learning phonics. I'm thrilled when they associate sounds with letters and groups of letters. Reggie learns words by breaking them down into letter sounds, while Kathy learns words as a whole. After consonants, we make word patterns by rhyming.

"Roam, gnome . . . home," Kathy says.

"Suck, luck, fuck," Reggie says.

I hate to leave, mid-afternoon.

"Will you come back to teach us to read more words?" Kathy says.

"I hope so, with library materials you can use," I say. "After I finish my study."

"When?" she says. She clutches Reggie.

"In a few months," I say. "Would you like to keep your three-by-five cards?"

"Nah," Reggie says. He turns away.

I'm depressed the whole way back to the library. A few months must seem forever to people not used to deferred gratification. I may never see Reggie and Kathy again.

"Girl," Vanessa says when she sees my teary eyes. "If you're going to be a wuss about this homeless proposal, I'm going to make you do six months in Cataloging."

After work, I go to the Ritz-Carlton to a women's networking cocktail hour. Vanessa used her considerable influence to get me into the group so that I could go instead of her. Networking is the business solution to a spiritual crisis.

After Reggie and Kathy, this meeting is culture shock. A few women here drink fizzy water, but most don't want to hold a glass that will make their handshakes cold. Two of them simultaneously introduce me to Gigi.

"We've met," Gigi and I say.

The two who introduced us peek furtively at each other's name tags and start gabbing together.

"I didn't know you were a member of this networking group," I say to Gigi.

"A client brought me," she says. "Don't blow my cover."

"What cover?"

"No one in networking has a past."

"Why not?"

"People don't want to know their image consultant grew up on a hog farm in Nebraska," she says.

"We used to have friends, now we have networks," I say.

"Who needs friends when we have clients?"

"What happened to all our old friends?" I say.

"They moved," she says. "You moved. I moved."

"Whatever happened to bonding?"

"Bonding peaks in college," she says. "We have only so much bonding in us and we used it up during our first few career moves. Besides, people bond only when they go through crises together."

"We still have plenty of crises."

"Not the kind we can tell a potential client," she says. "Tell me more about your sexual crisis, à la Princess Di."

But just as I'm about to, Barbara bears down on us.

"I love networking!" Barbara says. It's like farm-market day." She hugs us both at once.

I follow her gaze around the room. There is something festive about all these high-powered women trying to get each other to unburden their budgets.

"Everyone here is a consultant," Gigi says.

"We're not," I say.

"I'm a software consultant," she says. "Barbara's a financial consultant. You'd better consult about something or no one will take you seriously."

Three schools of networkers swim toward us, sweeping Gigi, Barbara, and me apart.

"What type of consulting do you do, Emily?" I say to a tall woman in a red suit, using a networking conversation generator.

"I'm a transition coach," she says.

"What type of transition?" I say.

"All kinds," she says. "Everyone's in transition these days—divorce, downsizing, retirement, pregnancy."

"Have you identified your client base?"

"I have so many clients I'm expanding my staff three hundred percent and moving into corner offices at Transco Tower."

"Really?" I say. "What are your qualifications?"

"I went through all the transitions myself at once. I got divorced just as I was about to be downsized, but I took early retirement instead because I discovered I was pregnant with triplets."

"Oh," I say.

"This is Dana, my business development coach," Emily says when another woman joins us. "I owe my success to her."

"It's all marketing," Dana says. She introduces me to Linda, her marketing strategist.

"Marketing and accounting," Linda says. She introduces me to Beth, her C.P.A.

"What do you do?" Beth asks me.

"I'm a homeless consultant."

She stares at me. "We've never had a consultant in our group who was homeless," she says, "but we like diversity."

I slip away in a blizzard of business cards. Cellular phones ring all over the room; women interrupt their conversations to answer them.

"They're all calling each other," Gigi says, when she sees I'm the only other person not on the phone.

"All the women I met were transition coaches, marketing strategists, or accountants," I say.

"Did you meet the ropes course facilitator?" she says.

"That's a subspecialty of one of the transition coaches."

"I thought she was a business development coach."

"They're all doing the same sorts of things for each other," I say. "Who's left to network *to,* when they're all preaching to the choir?"

"You have to get the library staff to a corporate team-building retreat," she says.

"Can you see me depending on Ralph, the bookmobile librarian, to get me from one tree to another on a trapeze?" I say. "Or pushing Vanessa over a twenty-foot wall?"

"It would enhance communication by building trust."

"It would destroy it altogether," I say.

"What I want to know is do these networkers make any money," she says.

"Tons, " I say. "I got invited to a Creative Money Visualization seminar."

"But did you network?" she says. "Did you increase your client base?"

"I didn't meet any homeless people here."

"Networkers are in their own economy," Gigi says. "One of them got a huge divorce settlement, and the rest are recycling her money."

7

Revenge of the Debutantes

On Saturday morning, Gabriel and I drive to Fort Worth for a debutante cotillion his parents have invited us to. I'm a wreck at the prospect of meeting his parents, Peaches and King, for the first time. His mother already disapproves of me for living with Gabriel outside the bonds of a society wedding. "You must be Gabriel's housekeeper," she said the first time she got me on the phone. "I'm his paramour," I said.

We stop at a red light before we get on the freeway. A homeless man directs traffic like a policeman. He wears a cardboard sign that reads "Hungry—Will Work For Food." Will Peaches think of me like that "Hungry—Will Work For Love"?

"You haven't told me about last weekend at the christening with your family," Gabriel says as we drive north on I-45. "How was it?"

"It was okay," I say.

Traffic rushes by us on both sides. In Texas, everyone passes you if you drive the speed limit.

"When will you take me to meet your family?" Gabriel says.

Keeping him from meeting them seems crucial to resolving my sexual anxiety. The more deeply I fall in love with Gabriel, the louder the shouts of protest from my Oedipal entourage.

Just then, a woman in a car by herself cuts us off. "Just Married" is scribbled on her windshield.

"Some people don't even carry mandatory accident insurance," I say.

"I have to get a new car anyway," Gabriel says when he realizes I'm not going to answer his question.

"What kind will you get?"

"One that's manly but not macho, reliable but good-looking, safe but not dull, fast but not a gas-guzzler, sporty but not flashy," he says.

"That car doesn't exist."

"It's out there," he says. "I'll find it."

Why not? He's manly, reliable, handsome, and sporty, and I found *him.* As far as I can tell, what's most important to him are antilock brakes. "Antilock brakes are miraculous," I say. "But no brakes can compensate for human error."

Gabriel sits tall in the pickup's leather seat. He holds the steering wheel as lightly as reins. He adjusts his cowboy hat against the bright Texas sun, sends his mind out with his herd to roam the range.

"What happens at this cotillion we're going to with your parents?" I say. "What *is* a cotillion, anyway?"

"Cocktails at seven, dinner at eight, presentation of the debutantes at nine."

"What debutantes?"

"They come out on the ballroom stage one at a time and make this bow," he says. "They have to touch their foreheads to the floor."

"No!"

"What does *debutante* mean to you?"

"Fairy princess."

"Means her daddy pays a lot of money to buy the right escorts and get her married off," he says.

I'm depressed. A dozen beautiful eighteen-year-olds in luscious white evening gowns who can touch their foreheads to the floor, all with rich parents. "Nobody can bend over and touch her forehead to the floor," I say. "Even I can't do it, and I've had ten years of yoga."

"I guarantee these girls don't do yoga."

"Are they in school or do they work, or what?"

"Partying's their job," he says. "Brunches, luncheons, teas, dinner-dances, late-night breakfasts. Bloody Marys, white wine, sherry, champagne, Mimosas. And they have to look good in spite of it."

"Everybody has to go to college," I say.

"They take the semester off to come out."

"Were you an escort?" I'm stricken with jealousy.

"Mother made me do it," he says. "Christmas I'd have to go to twenty deb parties. Inside the invitation was the name of the young lady I had to escort."

"Who paired you up?"

"The Fort Worth Dating Register," he says. "It's all mergers and acquisitions."

Finally we drive through the stone-pillared entry to Fort Worth's Westover Hills, up the winding streets canopied with big old trees, lush green lawns rolling away on both sides. The sign that says "Use Lower Drive for All Deliveries" seems a warning meant for me. I gasp at the enormous topiary armadillos on either side of the front door of his parents' mansion.

Gabriel's beautifilly groomed mother rushes out like the tornado that blew Dorothy to Oz. She's a tiny blonde in big hair and Chanel everything.

"*I've* heard such *won*derful *things* about you!" she says, throwing her diminutive self headlong into her favorite syllables.

"You have?" I say. I look at Gabriel.

He shrugs.

She pulls us into the long foyer. It looks like a gallery, but the pictures are at baseboard level, too low to see.

"Our cat loves art," Peaches says.

"Particularly Picasso's mice," Gabriel says.

The Benedicts' home is bigger than a homeless shelter but smaller than the housing project I grew up in. Room after room has no apparent purpose but entertaining guests—marble floors, high ceilings, flocked wallpaper, murals of Confederate battles. The brocaded French sofas look made for fainting on at the displays of china and silver in the antique hautboys. I'd love a tour but I don't know where to buy my ticket.

"Come, darlings," Peaches says when she catches me taking in all the gold-framed photos of Gabriel with Felicity—their rehearsal dinner, their wedding, their first Christmas with Gabe. "We have to be at my beauty salon in fifteen minutes."

"Mother," Gabriel says.

"This is the salon where Commander Schweppes has *his* beard trimmed," she says, and tugs Gabriel's. "Colleen can have my appointment with Donny because I'm just getting a comb-out."

"What's a comb-out?" Gabriel asks me as his mother races off to get her car.

"It's something ladies get," I say.

I looked fine to myself before we got there, but Peaches makes me feel raggedy and grateful to be taken in hand. We jump into her idling Mercedes. Even I can tell the idle is set high. Peaches makes Gabriel scrunch into the child-size back seat of her 500 SL, giving me the front bucket seat beside her. "But he's a doctor," I say.

"I'm his *mother*," she says.

"Where's Father?" Gabriel asks her.

"At the office," she says. "You know how he loves to work."

"But this is Saturday," I say.

"That's what's so cute about it," she says. "We get some little thing like the air-conditioning bill in the morning mail and he runs out to make more money."

At Ba-Ba-Boom Beauty, a valet parks Peaches's Mercedes. The place is in an uproar of shampooists, stylists, makeup artists, petulant manicurists. Three guys fall on us, clicking their scissors. We stand at the appointment desk while Peaches arbitrates who's going to get Gabriel's beard.

"Don't let them take off too much," I tell him. "Whatever happens, don't let them shave off your whole beard. We don't know how much your mother has bribed this hair-dresser."

Gabriel looks imperious and disdainful at the implication that he would do what either his mother or I wished.

"This isn't like going to the barber's," I say. I wring my hands. "They're going to give you one of those San Francisco piss-elegant beards."

He's led off by a hairdresser in leather chaps.

"What are we going to do to you?" Donny, the stylist who got me, says. He picks up and drops chunks of my hair.

"We're going to a cotillion," I say. Someone hands me a

china demitasse of espresso with a little lemon twist.

"So you need to look—hot," he says.

"I guess," I say. I look like Rebecca of Sunnybrook Farm.

Donny sighs and hands me over to a shampooist while he dashes out for a snort of coke.

On my way back to Donny's station, I pass Gabriel's beard being swept up by the hairdresser in chaps. "Where is he?" I say.

"Being blown *dry*."

Donny rolls me on some hot ones. "Let them cool their jets for a while," he says, and abandons me. I meditate, calmly noting my mind-states of helplessness and panic. Donny comes and goes, feels my rollers. Peaches comes and goes too, but I can't hear what she says above the Euro-disco and blowdryers. She's on her fourth cup of espresso. Her comb-out done, she ensconces herself nearby like the Queen Mother.

"Are we up today?" Donny asks her as he unrolls me.

"Very," Peaches says. "I come here when I don't have time to see my doctor," she tells me. "Donny and I have a buddy system."

Across the salon, Gabriel paces back and forth, his beard a shadow of its former self. I can't tell whether he's trying to see what they're doing to me, or pleading to be rescued.

"Why didn't you come over?" I ask him when we're through and Peaches signs a bill as big as the national debt.

"Didn't want to get involved," he says.

I mourn for his beard. "Do you do tattoos?" I snap at the receptionist.

"It'll grow," Gabriel says as we wait for the car.

"How could you let them do it to you?" I ask him. "I thought you thought it was unmanly to go into a place like that."

"A man can go anywhere," he says.

Peaches has put us in separate rooms, but who can make love in his parents' house, anyway? My pink guest room has a four-poster canopy bed, imposing portraits of several Texan generals, chamber pots brimming with magnolia blossoms, and an enormous gold harp.

Gabriel knocks on the door of my room. "Dalzenia's waiting to iron your dress for the cotillion," he says.

"Dalzenia who?"

"Mother's maid."

"It doesn't need to be ironed." Vanessa lent me her best Oscar de la Renta ballgown, a rich ruby satin cascading with ruffles.

"You have to let her iron it," he says. "It's part of how Mother 'does for' people."

"How's that, if Dalzenia's going to iron it?"

"Dalzenia does the work, and Mother gets the credit."

This peek into class relations makes me dizzy. "I'll iron it myself," I say. I grew up ironing, hot summer afternoons in the project.

"You won't be able to find the ironing board," he says. "It's in some part of the house no one but Dalzenia's ever been."

I watch my dress on its satin hanger go from Gabriel to Peaches to Dalzenia. I surreptitiously follow Dalzenia through the dining room and kitchen, then through a maze of little pantries lined with shelves of glassware, china, cookware, canned goods, preserves. If lose her, I'll never find my way out. She finally comes to a stop in a laundry room with two washers and dryers, the ironing board, and more cleaning products than were ever mentioned in "Hints from Heloise."

"Lord!" Dalzenia says when she turns around and sees me.

"I'm sorry," I say, "I didn't mean to scare you."

Dalzenia is an imposing African-American woman in a starched white maid's uniform, the buttons straining across her formidable bosom. Her thick black hair, streaked with gray, is piled on top of her head and held in place with a hairnet with sparkles in it. Her face is smooth except for fierce frown-lines in her forehead and fiercer laugh-lines around her mouth.

"Go on and git, baby," she says. "I ain't going to steal your dress."

"It's just I'm not accustomed to having someone wait on me."

"Baby, you better get used to it 'cause ain't nobody do nothing around here but me."

"I'm Colleen Sweeney," I say. "I'm pleased to meet you."

"I know who you *is*." She winks. "Who is it you planning to *be*?"

So she's the architect I have to clear my designs on Gabriel with. "Is that a rhetorical question?"

She grins. "How's my little boy?"

"He's fine," I say, when I realize she means Gabriel. "Busy, but everything's okay."

"And how's the baby? How much his daddy got him?"

"First, third, and fifth weekends. Vacations too, of course."

"He adjusted to it?"

"Gabe's a flexible little boy," I say. "He's adjusted to it as well as can be expected."

"I mean his daddy."

"It's a difficult situation all around," I say.

"I know it *is*," she says. "I know it."

I don't know what to say. I hear Peaches calling me from far away in the white people's part of the house.

"You better go on or it won't be pretty," Dalzenia says.

"I hope we can talk again soon."

Dalzenia just shakes her head.

Dressed for the cotillion, I perch on an antebellum chair between our two rooms and wait for Gabriel.

"What are you doing?" he says when he comes out of his in his tux.

"Being good and not getting dirty."

We go downstairs in our formal attire.

"Howdy," Gabriel's father, King, says to me.

King is heavy-set in his tux, his starched white shirt a vast expanse as bleached as the Texas plains. His cowboy hat is the most tasteful one I've ever seen—platinum-colored with a trim roll to the brim and a conservative crown, but soft and silky in 100X beaver at least. He wears handmade black python boots.

Peaches looks created by Christian Lacroix.

"Don't you feel seedy next to us since you missed Ba-Ba-Boom Beauty?" she says to King.

"How do you like what they did to you?" King asks me.

My hair is a leaning tower of curls. "I think it makes me look Southern," I say.

"She looks Prussian," King says to Peaches.

"King thinks everything Prussian is wonderful," Peaches says to me, but I'm not so sure.

"Let's get this over with, Mother," Gabriel says.

"Let the children take the Jaguar and we'll take the Mercedes," Peaches says to King. "If we all go in the Jaguar, the valets will think we have only one car and it'll be all over town by morning."

"Peaches," King says.

King drives the Mercedes even faster than Peaches does. Gabriel has a hard time keeping up in the Jaguar.

The gold and white ballroom glows like a movie set, with hundreds of candlelit tables and chandeliers. The society orchestra plays. Tons of cleavage dance by.

"What a paradox," I say to Gabriel. "The introduction of virgins to proper society in this sea of opulence and seduction."

Gabriel and King pin a tiny piece of red ribbon on their lapels. It's like half of an AIDS ribbon, but it's to show they're members and they paid.

"You do your best mixing before dinner," Peaches says, and tugs us from little group to group. I can't extricate myself from conversations, but Peaches has the gift of walking away in the middle of somebody's sentence and nobody minds. She works a crowd better than anyone I've ever seen.

"You look mighty pretty this evening," Gabriel says to one friend of his mother after another, before turning to talk with the men in a gentlemanly way about cars. "Is it turbo?" he says.

I study the ladies to make note of what works—bare shoulders, lots of jewels, couture everything. This is my idea of heaven, everyone dressed up as her best self with beautiful manners. I feel like Jezebel in my red ruffles.

"Everyone is so nice," I say to Gabriel. "They *like* me here."

"Have to be nice, or the Southern hospitality police would give them one upside the head," he says.

"In the Northeast, people are supposed to frown when they meet you," I say.

"How do you know whether they like you?"

"That's the purpose of etiquette, to keep everyone off balance."

When Gabriel can't stand mixing another second, he runs off and comes back with my dance card. He writes his name in all the spaces. He ties the card's white ribbon to my wrist, the little white pencil dangling. Then he points discreetly to his mouth—if he doesn't eat soon, awful things will happen. We head for our table, Peaches calling after us. I turn around and wave. If I marry Gabriel, serious as he is, Peaches will see to it I have fun. She makes her way toward our table, nodding and waving to her friends as if from a float in a parade.

"I was just about to call nine-one-one," Gabriel says when dinner is served. Tiny barbecued shrimp, tender medallions of something, artistic vegetables, a lot of plate.

King is seated on my left. "Where do your people come from, Colleen?" he says.

"Boston, Massachusetts," I say. In Texas I always feel I have to tell people where Boston is.

"That's a lot of wagon-wheel greasin's from here," he says.

"Tell me about your ranch," I say.

"It's pretty country," he says, "except for a number of big, ugly but mighty profitable oil wells."

"Do you spend a lot of time there?" I say.

"Business keeps me in town most of the time, but the foreman keeps it running," he says. "Ranching's the best way to make a living there is, *if* you can make a living. Way to do it is inherit thirty thousand acres, put some sheep and hogs on it, and a few cattle for status."

How do King, Peaches, and Gabriel fit into family systems theory?

"How do you inherit thirty thousand acres?" I ask Gabriel.

"Pick the right parents," he says.

The cotillion is all about family, the jewel in society's crown. Who would I be now if I'd been the adored daughter in a beautiful family? I study the satin-covered Programme with the portraits of the debutantes. They look like a perfected species from another planet.

"Our interest for the evening is Miss Louisa Wilton," Peaches says to me. "The Wiltons are our dearest friends."

"Peaches has hundreds of dearest friends," King says.

"And they're all here," she says, phosphorescent in her makeup.

My understanding of makeup seems hypothetical by comparison. I feel like a nun with a beautician's degree. I study the little biographical sketch of Miss Wilton, great-great-great-grandaughter of General Josiah Samuel Wilton. She's a seventh-generation Texan, member of the handbell choir and the National Huguenot Society, and plans to major in sociology in college.

"What business is your daddy in?" King asks me.

Gabriel leans in to hear my response.

"He took early retirement," I say. "Very early."

"He must be mighty successful," King says.

After pecan balls smothered in hot fudge, the debutantes come out, one by one. We hold our breath as each shakily bows in her high heels, sinks into the swirl of her full skirt, dips her bare shoulders. Her escort appears, folds her gloved arm into his. No one could get up from that bow without help.

Miss Wilton is a vision of the prosperous innocence I've always aspired to. "What's that mean, she's our 'interest'?" I ask Gabriel.

"Our horse." He looks like a man who lost big at the races. Is he thinking of Felicity?

"Do you have horses?" I say to King.

"I do," he says, "and a quarterhorse who's the best I've ever had for working cattle. A horse is like a husband. If you don't like him, you ought not to still have him."

The orchestra strikes up some fanfare. The deb and her escort promenade the length of the ballroom.

"Don't you want to marry one of these girls instead of getting involved with me?" I say to Gabriel.

"I already did," he says.

Felicity was a debutante, of course. My left shoulder pad slips out of the dress I borrowed from Vanessa. That's the trouble with shoulder pads, they don't stay on if your shoulders are small enough to need them. I slip it into my evening bag and hope no one thinks I'm stealing the silver.

"Was Peaches a debutante?" I ask King.

"Peaches was Maid of Oil," he says. "That's top debutante."

"Isn't this *fuuuun*," Peaches says.

"I could understand my being here if I were a social climber," I say to Gabriel.

"You're better off learning deeper values from the homeless," he says.

The Grand March begins. The debs parade with their escorts around the dance floor, then break into a waltz. Candlelight flashes on their faces.

"Here come the bill-payers," Gabriel says, as the debutantes' fathers cut in.

The escorts ask the girls' mothers to dance.

"This is so Freudian," I say.

King and Peaches get up to dance.

Gabriel stares at the debutante pageantry as if into a box

already emptied, knowing he got everything in there but disappointed anyway. It's the revenge of the debutantes.

I place my hand on his. "I love you," I say.

He smiles at me, then checks the dance card on my wrist. "It says right here I have this dance."

8

Leave It Right Where Jesus Flang It

The next morning, I have a hard time extricating myself from the deep flounces of the canopied four-poster. I peer out from layers of white eyelet to meet the stern stare of Colonel William Barret Travis, commander of the Alamo. Engraved on the gold plate beneath his portrait are the words "I shall never surrender or retreat."

I dress and go downstairs to the breakfast room. Peaches sits at the antique table, herself a white-eyelet vision in a beribboned floor-length dressing gown.

"How're you, Colleen?" she says, over the roar of Sunday-morning TV.

"Fine, thank you," I say. "How're you?"

"It doesn't matter," she says. "Will you have a Mimosa?"

She's drinking what looks like two-hundred-proof black coffee. I opt for herbal tea.

Dalzenia pushes through the swinging door and clears a table space for me among several Texas newspapers and the *New York Times*. She looks unused to dealing with yuppie needs but capable of producing some herbal tea even if she has to grow and harvest it herself.

"Gabriel went to church with his daddy," Peaches says. "Church is a comfort to them, poor things."

I like this milieu where the men go to church and the women stay home and put their feet up.

"Can we do some girl talk?" Peaches says. She puts down her newspaper and leans toward me.

I must look petrified, because Dalzenia brings us a couple of Mimosas. So far I've evaded Peaches and King's questions about my family, not to mention Gabriel's pressure to reciprocate by inviting him to Boston.

"Why isn't Gabriel wearin' his Rolex?" Peaches says, instead.

"What Rolex?"

"The one his daddy and me gave him when he graduated from medical school."

"Oh, *that* Rolex." I've never seen Gabriel wear any but his black plastic altimeter watch. It's not much use in Houston, but I've caught him looking at it hopefully when we go up and down in elevators. "Why don't you ask him?"

"I couldn't. There are some things a mother can't ask her son."

She looks so crestfallen I wish there were something I could do to help. I've learned that things mean things down South they don't up North. "Probably Felicity got it in the divorce."

"That beeitch," she says. "Do excuse me. It's just I worry it means Gabriel's depressed."

"His work in the emergency room takes a toll," I say. "Although he loves it, in his way."

"Course it does," she says. "I always wanted him to go into something cheerful, like plastic surgery. Even if he hated the work, he could have loved the money. Although as a boy he wouldn't do chores for money because he didn't care about spending it. I made him read the Sears, Roebuck catalog until he found something he wanted to buy."

"That worked," I say. "He loves catalogs now."

"Gabriel preferred bein' gloomy even as a little boy," she says. "I had him in elocution, French lessons, polo, archery, violin. Left to his own devices, he would have just played in his sandbox."

If Gabriel weren't in his thirties, I'd get him a sandbox for his birthday. "He'll feel better when he's over his divorce," I say. "Am I different from Felicity?"

"You wouldn't ever choose the same flatware pattern."

"Oh."

"There's nothing wrong with Felicity a good spankin' wouldn't fix," she says. "Of course I mean thirty years ago. Felicity has the Terrible Two's at thirty-two."

"A spankin'?"

"Why don't I buy y'all a membership in a Houston country club and you could get out and meet some people, have some fun," she says. "I'll do it with the next dividend I get through my investment club."

"You belong to an investment club?"

"It's just a fun group of ladies who got together to rebuild the Texas economy," she says. "We are making so much money in tips."

"Tips?" I say.

She pours me another Mimosa, mostly champagne with just a hint of orange juice. "The conservative investors get them from their horoscopes, but the risk-takers like me get them from our massage therapists," she says. "Once a month at our tea we have an intuition blow-out, big-time. Don't tell the men because it might hurt their feelings to find out where the smart money is."

•

King and Gabriel come home from church, and here I am plastered in the middle of the day. I feel like a debutante.

"Maybe I'd better have some coffee," I say to Peaches.

"That's a myth about coffee sobering you up after," she says. "You have to drink the coffee *before*."

The four of us take our places in the lovely glass-walled dining room. Peaches has place cards for brunch. She has given me the best view of the elaborate gardens, lush with bright red hibiscus. In the center of the manicured green lawn is an Olympic-sized, Texas-shaped pool, the diving board over Fort Worth. The pool water is the most exquisite aquamarine I've ever seen.

"Gazing at that color blue is supposed to be good for your fifth chakra," I say to Gabriel. I wonder if he can tell how tipsy I am.

"You out of your mind?"

"Did you say a prayer for me?" I ask him. Say a little prayer for me, my father used to say as I left for church in my little white gloves and hat.

"I did," he says, "but it doesn't seem to have done you any good." King and Gabriel create the same united front against flighty, irresponsible women that Gabriel and Gabe do.

After King says grace, Dalzenia serves us each a rum-glazed plum in a nest of strawberries.

"Church must have done you some good," I say to Gabriel. "What was the sermon about?" People like me who don't go to church always want to know about the sermon from the people who went. It's partly to get the good of church without having to sit through it, but mostly to confirm our wisdom in not going in the first place.

"The sermon was an exhortation to contribute monetarily, generously, and frequently to our less fortunate brethren," King says.

I stab my plum with my fruit fork, cut off the side with my fruit knife, while King and Gabriel discuss the tithe one should give to the church and charities. Dalzenia cuts the quiche and I see a pie chart divided into save-the-this and save-the-that, foreign missions, poverty programs, environmental rescues, and various educational and philanthropic organizations.

"We have to give ten, fifteen percent of our income to even begin to meet the need," Gabriel says.

"Gabriel doesn't want things for himself," Peaches says to me. "For me, if a little is good, more is better."

King says a couple of people in the congregation oppose spending church donations on social causes. "They'd pull you out of the crick if you were drownin'," he says. "Trouble is, they haven't got the ability to handle ideas. They got animosity and rancor against women, homosexuals, blacks, all minorities."

They converse so cautiously I can't find my way in. In my family, we'd all be yelling at each other by now. We take social problems as personal attacks.

"Right-wingers?" I say.

"Aren't those the people who believe *every word* of the Bible?" Peaches says.

"An African-American man I dated once subscribed to the Bible," I say. "But he was hardly a right-winger."

"Beg pardon?" King says. He holds his fork midair.

Peaches puts down her coffee cup. Gabriel stares at me. Only Dalzenia retains her composure.

"He was a tax attorney," I say. "We went to the symphony. It was in Boston."

"Of course," Peaches says in a get-the-smelling-salts voice.

King wrenches the subject away. "Yup," he says. "If you see three-toed tracks and eight-inch holes in your lawn or flower beds, you probably got a problem with armadillos."

"Tell them how you catch them, King," Peaches says after a moment, her impeccable hostessing skills coming to the rescue.

"Run after 'em," he says. "Best time is when it's cold, say forty degrees. Armadillos can't run too well when it's cold. The armadillo gets winded before me and I just pick it up in my bare hands."

"Tell them what you *do* when you catch them."

"Send 'em to a laboratory doing research on leprosy and birth defects," he says. "Now if I see one that looks sick, I don't pick it up."

"Bless his heart," Peaches says.

Outside the floor-to-ceiling glass walls, the Benedicts' dog paces up and down. A large golden retriever, he watches us with the same plaintive look of my mother's golden retriever, Humphrey. I picture my mother having breakfast in Boston by herself—instant coffee, toast with grape jelly. When we lived in the project, she'd send my brother or me to the store on Sunday morning for a box of powdered-sugar doughnuts. We didn't feel deprived of anything; we had everything we knew we wanted. Is poverty relative? Only to a certain point, beyond which people like Chance know they're suffering.

I sip from my crystal goblet of ice water. "Do our country's problems stem from race or class?" I say.

Dalzenia stops serving. Peaches and King stare at one another.

"Or both?" I say.

No armadillos come to my rescue.

"Neither?" I say.

I look at Gabriel. He stares down at his plate.

"I've never understood why Gabriel insists on takin' care of poor people!" Peaches says finally. "Why doesn't he like rich people, who'd pay him what he deserves?" She stands, throws down her damask napkin, runs from the table.

I'm completely confused. How did we get from race and class to Peaches's rage at Gabriel for working in the E.R.?

King blots his mouth with his napkin, rises, and follows Peaches.

Gabriel stands also, goes upstairs to get our luggage.

I sit for a moment in the ruins.

Before we leave, I slip into the kitchen to find Dalzenia.

Surrounded by dirty dishes and the remains of Sunday brunch, she watches a Sunday televangelist on a small TV. "They're taking money away from poor people in the name of God," she says.

"They're being bad," I say. But not as bad as me, more upsetting than Princess Di.

"God told me to tell you this and God told me to tell you that," she fusses at the televangelist. "God told you to tell me nothin'!"

I watch it with her a few minutes, until she turns it off in disgust.

"Dalzenia," I say, "what do you think would solve the homeless problem?"

"It'd take someone starting over to raise each of them up right."

"What about crime?" I say. "What about drugs?"

"I don't understand none of it no more, hon'," she says. "The world is moving too fast on me. That's why I quit watching TV except for Sunday. They put anything on there. Don't have no respect for anyone. So many people getting killed or raped." She throws a handful of flatware into the sink.

I hold the garbage bag while she empties trash into it.

"Do you he'p your own maid?" she says.

"I don't have a maid."

"Who do your cleaning?"

"I'm Irish," I say. "Cleaning is my hobby."

"Didn't you have a maid when you was coming up?"

"No," I say. "I had to take care of the house, my younger brother, and myself while my mother worked."

"Gabriel and them have always had help."

"Have you worked here your whole life?" I say. Together we carry a heavy stack of silver platters to the kitchen counter.

"I came here when Gabriel was a baby," she says. "They had a lot more help then, and my husband Leroy was the yard man. All of them are dead except me."

"What was your husband like?"

Her eyes well with tears.

"I'm sorry, Dalzenia."

"I got me a man-friend," she says. "He don't make a living but he make living worthwhile." She rinses and dries the silver teapot, then gets out the cloths to polish it and the trays and flatware.

I reel from all the things I've learned about Gabriel and his parents. It's not just that Gabriel likes church, but that race relations down South are so different from up North.

Suddenly, the museum-quality African jar on top of the refrigerator begins to shake. It rocks back and forth, slowly at first, then faster and faster. Paralyzed, we watch it fall to the floor and shatter into a hundred pieces.

The cat who loves art emerges unscathed from the wreckage.

"Was that really so wrong," I say as we pick up the shards, "to bring up race and class?"

"Baby," Dalzenia says, "I'm goin' to leave that right where Jesus flang it."

9

Help Me, I'm Your Father

Gabriel sits in stony silence the whole drive back to Houston from Fort Worth.

"I know I blew it with your parents," I say, not to mention how I blew it with him. "It must have been the Mimosas talking. At least I didn't tell them I once did exotic dancing."

The truth is, most of what I know about fitting in with wealthy people I learned from Web. He'd get us seated at the captain's table on his cruise ship, so I could practice on the ambassador to my left, the countess to my right. Sometimes these were the people hosting the orgy after dinner, so I learned to be sensitive to a variety of social cues.

"No one's fighting for justice for exotic dancers," he says.

"What was so terrible about bringing up race and class?"

"We don't talk politics in polite company."

"Where else is it safe to fight about it?"

"We don't fight!"

"From the tone of your voice," I say, "I ought to get out of the pickup and walk home."

"I can explain it to you," he says, "but I can't understand it for you."

"Politics isn't about itself," I say. "In my family, it's about ourselves, our place in the family."

"In my family, one's place is predetermined," he says. "Even before we're born."

No wonder Peaches is obsessed with place cards. "Your mother disapproves of your social conscience," I say. "She'd rather you be a party wherever you go."

He glares at me. "Don't say squat about my mother!"

"She said squat about *you*. I'm on your side."

"Those are two different buckets of possums," he says. He floors the gas pedal down I-45.

We roar past the huge white statue of Sam Houston, president of the Republic of Texas. Towering over the freeway, he frowns down at me. How do I make things so much worse for myself without even trying?

"If your parents don't fight," I say when we walk into Gabriel's apartment, "how do they know what they disagree about before it leads to divorce?"

"They'd never divorce," he says. "If they think about killing each other, they do it privately."

"I was raised to believe if I jumped over the broomstick and didn't like it, I could jump back over the other way."

"I couldn't marry a woman who doesn't take marriage seriously."

"But you yourself are divorced," I say.

He ducks his head. His broad shoulders slump. "I could never go through it again."

The nanoseconds have been ticking by since early June when I moved in. Now it's late September. "We've been living together for four months," I say. "What if I'm your Ms. Wrong?"

"That's for me to decide," he says. "Your job is to figure out whether I'm your Dr. Right."

I'm staring at him when the phone rings.

It's an emergency room doctor in Boston. "Dehydration and malnutrition," he says. My father's in the hospital.

"Is he dying?"

"He's in bad shape," the doctor says. "He could get worse in a hurry."

I throw clothes to hang around a hospital in into my carry-on bag, as well as a black dress in case he dies.

"Where are you going?" Gabriel says.

"My father's in the hospital."

"I'm coming with you."

"No," I say. How can I let him meet my father at his worst?

"I've just taken you to meet my parents. Clearly it's time I meet yours."

But the gap between the classes has widened to an abyss.

"No," I say again.

I leave Gabriel looking as if he just found a rattler in his bedroll.

I fly to my father like a yuppie Mary Poppins, catapulting out of Houston's late September humidity into Boston's autumn. The sharp blue sky, the crisp reds of bricks and leaves leave me at one remove, distant and anxious. My heart actually hurts from fighting with Gabriel. At least it feels like a fight—Gabriel's aristocratic manners make it hard to tell. I feel as if I've been fighting and he hasn't. When I most need to make up with Gabriel, my father is pulling me away.

I have to go to him, but I don't have the emotional cog to take care of my father. They took it when they took out my tonsils.

The city hospital is a little city, with its parking garage, gift shop, cafeteria, newsstand, pay phones, restrooms, so many people rushing here and there. I ride up in the elevator with a doctor. Doctors have a certain look even when they're not in whites—more focused than visitors, more relaxed than residents or interns, as if they're on their way back to their seats after intermission. I already miss Gabriel. Will I have to get used to it? My father's being homeless is just one of the differences between us.

Propped up in bed, my unshaven father stares unhappily into the hall. He shares a room with an emaciated boy who has the window side. A nurse comes in and closes the curtain between them.

"The fellow in the next bed has AIDS," my father whispers. "He needs the view."

I hug him, in his blue and white nightgown printed with "Hospital Property." He's hooked up to two intravenous machines with so many bells and whistles it's as if he has two robots for guardian angels.

There's no chair so I sit on the portable commode. "How do you feel, Dad?"

"I can't poop," he says. "My stomach doesn't work anymore because everything I've eaten is still in there."

"Like bad karma."

"The doc says it's like not running a garbage disposal," he says. "It's not good for the garbage to just rot."

"What medical coverage do you have?"

"I don't know," he says. "I don't like to go sticking my nose into it."

"How much Social Security do you get each month?"

"Well, it's like this," he says. "Not much, because Social Security overpaid me for years and now I have to pay them back."

"What do you mean, they overpaid you?"

"Their computer thought I put in more than I did."

"You're the only indigent person I know who *owes* Social Security!"

"Try not to hate me, honey," he says.

We sit and sulk for a few minutes. The AIDS patient in the next bed plays a cassette of Barbra Streisand singing "People who need people" over and over again.

"He plays that all day," my father says.

My father's an imp—an incompetent nincompoop. Why does my hold on life depend on someone else's being wrong? "You got dehydrated?" I say. "You didn't eat?"

"There's no water where I stay," he says. "No gas or electricity to cook with."

"Why not?"

"Nobody lives there."

"You live there," I say.

"Not really."

"You hole up in an abandoned building," I say. "You're still homeless?"

He sighs so big I feel a draft, as they say in Texas. "You have a bad way of putting things, honey."

I sit there while he tries to muster the energy to explain. If I lose Gabriel, I'll refuse to want anything anymore. I'm happiest when I don't want something; there's so much I don't want. What I didn't bring to Gabriel's or put in storage, I gave away. I'm walking into nothingness by half-lives. Things, people, feelings.

"I rented a room from Hazel Johnson who owned the house," my father says after a while. "She got sick, and I took care of her. She died. You won't believe this, but she left me her house."

"You own the house?"

"Hazel's relatives are crawling out of the woodwork, saying it's theirs. They never even came to visit her; now they say I forced her to give it to me."

"They're contesting her will?"

"I don't have any money for a legal hullabaloo." His shoulders collapse. "Meanwhile the house is going to pieces. I can't pay the utility bills or taxes; I can't afford fire insurance."

"If it burns down, it's worth only a fraction for the lot," I say. "Your support hangs on that house."

"You're afraid I'll be a burden."

"Are you trying to become one?"

"Don't push me," he says. "I've been trying to sort out Hazel's estate and I'll keep working on it."

"If you haven't done it by now, how are you going to when you're sick?"

"I just need time."

"You haven't *got* time," I say. "What are you going to live on?"

"Please," he says. "I can't deal with your crisis mentality."

"It's *your* crisis!"

"What do you want me to do?" He drops his head back on his pillow. One of his I.V. machines beeps wildly.

"What should I do?"

"Press the call button for the nurse," he gasps.

"You have your foot on the tubing," the nurse says to me when she rushes in.

"You're trying to pull the plug on me, honey," my father says.

"We didn't think he had any family," the nurse says.

"He's estranged," I say.

On the other side of the curtain, the brother of the boy with AIDS pleads with him to let him tell their parents. "Come home," he says.

"I can't do that to them," the boy moans.

"You have to give them a chance to forgive you," his brother says.

My mother got us out of the project when I was in high school, and moved to a tiny house. I stay at her house because it's closer to the hospital than Doug and Pamela's way out in the heavenly suburbs.

My mother's heart-shaped face is softening in her cheekbones, her chin. Her skin is clean and dry, all the whiter for the pale blue of her eyes.

We sit in the kitchen and eat tomato soup she made for me.

"What do you usually have for dinner?" I say.

"Cereal. Bite-sized Shredded Wheat if I have a coupon."

"Is that enough?"

"I like cereal," she says.

She eats as if she's still poor. We used to open the kitchen cabinets at dinnertime, make pancakes, whatever was there. I love to cook for Gabriel; I now have a three-week rotation of vegetarian recipes. I'd hate to go back to eating by myself.

"You need more than that," I say. I don't know how to show her I care about her without sounding critical. I'm still kicking myself for criticizing Gabriel's mother.

"I open a can of fruit cocktail if I'm still hungry."

"That's dessert."

"I have a martini for dessert," she says.

We sit there in silence. If I could figure out why I keep my father at one remove, could I understand why my mother does the same to me?

"Dad was suffering from malnutrition," I say after a while.

"Your father makes a mess of everything, then expects someone else to straighten it all out."

"He's sick."

"It's not serious. You know how he dramatizes things." My mother can't afford to care about my father anymore. He exhausted her resources.

"I made a list." I break crackers into my soup. "I'll talk to his doctor about what to expect. If he's going down the tubes, I'll ask his wishes about organ donation, burial, all that."

"No one would want his organs."

"If he makes it through this," I go on, "he'll need a visiting nurse and other services."

"Even if he recovers, he'll soon be back in the hospital with something else."

"Why doesn't he take care of his own affairs?" I say.

"He doesn't know how."

"He inherited the house he lives in from someone he took care of until she died."

"Artificial responsibilities were the only kind he assumed," she says.

"It's all tied up in legal complications."

"You'll have to ask Doug to help you."

"How can I?" I say. "He hates Dad."

"He's terrified of being like him,'" she says. "But he's not the kind of person who just says no."

Doug explodes when I call him. "I don't have much choice, do I!"

"Just tell me what to do and I'll do it."

"Get the damn documentation," he says. "Copy of the deed. Where it's recorded. Nature of the legal fight. Names and phone numbers of the attorneys. Receipts paid in connection with the property."

It sounds impossible. "If he has it, I'll get it."

"We'll have to run a title search, then unload the property to pay his damn debts," he says.

"Thanks, Doug. Our only alternative is to watch him collect cans in a shopping cart."

He hangs up on me.

"Doug's furious," I say to my mother.

"Well, I guess *so*," she says. "Your father never was a father to him. Here's this person Doug doesn't even like, who shows up saying 'Help me, I'm your father.'"

I lie in bed that night and remember how, as children, Dougie and I used to call to our father to bring us milk. "Warm milk, warm milk!" we mewed in unison from our beds. He got up naked to heat the milk in the cold kitchen and brought it to us, then we all went back to sleep.

Our father used to tell us we were going to go live on a houseboat in Maine. He was a hippie before it became a movement. He went everywhere on a bicycle after he lost his driver's license for drunk driving. He took Dougie and me for long rides in the bicycle's baby seat. He took us to beach amusement parks and bought us white sailor hats. Dougie and I wore our sailor hats when our father mowed the tall grass in the back yard, so he could see us as he waded through it with his scythe.

The next day, in a decaying neighborhood in South Boston, I find my father's abandoned house. It's an old brick rowhouse with dust-caked windows and cracks in the stoop. Paint flakes from the door when I push it open. I stand for a moment on the threshold. The house is oddly quiet, like my unit in the Buffalo Mini-Warehouses, stuffed cardboard cartons and brown grocery bags stacked to shoulder height. I feel I'm trespassing, as if the dead woman's ghost were still here.

My father's mattress lies on the floor, like Gabriel's futon.

Gabriel and I fit so well together in his bed. His warm breath on my neck, I nestled the curves of my back and buttocks into the front of his body, the angles of my legs into his. My breasts clasped in his large hand, we slept. I'm already mourning him in the past tense.

I glance at the open mail on my father's kitchen counter. Overdue tax bills and other alarming notices. A delinquent bill from the electric company and one of those questionnaires to determine hardship cases. "Is there a child in your household?" it reads. I open the refrigerator in case there are rotting perishables, but it's empty.

My father's daily horoscopes are outlined in red on old newspapers: "Today is a good day to make advances in your career"; "Your charisma attracts member of the opposite sex"; "New business opportunity calls for a short trip."

I read my own horoscope, weeks old. "You feel a certain individual does not deserve your time or attention," it says. "Swallow your pride to avoid further conflicts."

I lift a box from the top of the pile and empty it on the floor, start going through the contents. My father's boxes are full of what he took when he left us and what he has accumulated since. News clippings, obituaries, family snapshots. Crossword puzzles in various stages, articles obsessively saved from magazines. Some of the boxes have small household items in them—a toaster with a frayed cord, a broken ceramic figurine of a small boy.

Does Chance have cartons of stuff stashed somewhere? I messed up big-time. That's what Chance says of himself, but he doesn't let it drive him crazy the way I'm doing. By now, Gabriel must realize what my mistakes with his parents revealed—I'm not right for him. Has he already fallen out of love with me?

I'd asked my father whether his boxes were in any kind of order. "I don't know what to tell you, honey," he'd said. I come across his notebooks—dozens of them crammed with reminders to himself. Unable to organize his life, he tried instead to save the evidence of it. I find keys, none identified. In each box I find lottery tickets—a few at first, then fistfuls. Then shopping bags full of lottery stubs, thousands of dollars' worth.

I become an archivist of my father's papers. I find the court order that granted my mother her separation from my father. His visitation rights to see Dougie and me were stated as "Sunday from 1 P.M. to 5 P.M." Hours later, I find the legal correspondence alleging that Hazel Johnson's bequest of her house was procured by my father's "fraud and undue influence." I add it to the few receipts pertaining to the estate.

Tired and hungry, I grow disoriented, as if slipping off some edge. I'm in my father's broken-down house, coming to him from the inside out. His thrift-shop trousers, limp gray shirt, out-of-shape jacket hang over a chair. He might need his worn-out slippers at the hospital. I put them in my purse, just as Felicity did with Gabe's shoes.

"Whenever he got a bill from a lawyer, Dad just got a new lawyer," I tell Doug.

"That figures."

"I've put together a chronology of what happened, with approximate dates, lawyers' names, that sort of thing."

He growls.

"His doctor says his various problems are resolving for now," I say.

"I don't think much of doctors," he says. "They're just technicians."

I ache for Gabriel in the E.R., picking up the pieces of ruined lives, trying in the face of his dismay to put them back together.

I call him, to hear whether he's still angry with me, to say I'm sorry, to wait for him to say he misses me and wants me to come home. But all I get is our answering machine. All I hear is my own voice, saying we're not there.

"Did Dad always gamble?" I ask my mother.

"He was a numbers runner," she says, "but he wasn't good even at that. He drank away the money people paid him to place bets. More than once the bookies wanted to break his knees. We had to borrow hundreds of dollars to pay the bookies. Sometimes your father had to play all the numbers himself so he'd have the cash to pay any winners."

"He plays the lottery now."

"Why do you bother with him?" she says.

"I'm trying to help."

"You can't," she says. "I tried for years."

After my father left us, I painted two seashells with flowers, matching ashtrays for my mother's Happy Anniversary present. "Honey, it's like celebrating the day you got the measles," she said. But she still has the painted seashells.

"I'm trying to learn to love him, then," I say.

"I found an old apron I made for you out of one of your father's shirts."

"I remember it," I say. "It made me feel I belonged to both of you."

"If you *want* to love your father," she says, "you *do* love your father."

On my way to the airport, I stop at the hospital to see my father one more time. The boy with AIDS has died. His spirit hovers like the Angel of Unconditional Love.

My father's hospital bed rises and falls with big sighs.

"Is this bed alive?" I say.

"It's an air mattress," he says. "So I won't get bedsores."

"It inhales and exhales."

"If I kick the bucket after you leave, honey," he says, "don't feel bad—the important thing is you came to see me."

"I want to be here if you're dying. Make sure someone lets me know."

"I'm not afraid of dying."

"What do you think dying's like?"

"You lie down," he says. "You fold your hands on your chest. People come and stand around your bed."

"What kind of funeral do you want?"

"Something simple, honey. Just a mahogany casket with silver handles, a big grassy plot somewhere. A new suit to be buried in, with a button-down shirt and nice tie."

"How do you plan to pay for that?"

"I won't have to, I'll be dead!"

"I'm a member of a memorial society," I say. "They have my final instructions on file and I've already paid for my funeral."

"Ever since Brownies you liked clubs."

We sit, suspended in the room's stillness. Covered with corns and callouses, his feet stick out from his blanket. "I brought you your slippers," I say.

"We're on earth to love other people," he says. "Put that in my obsequy."

"You haven't done any planning your whole life. Now you hear your requiem and see me delivering your eulogy to thousands of mourners?"

"You want to get rid of me. Why don't you just pull the plug?"

"I'm not through with you yet," I say. "We have some loose ends to tie up. Otherwise, the rest of us will be so busy cleaning up the mess you left, we won't have time to think about what a great guy you were. We'll be too mad to grieve."

"If you don't bury me for love, you'll bury me for stink."

We sit and look at each other, on the bed that's rising and falling.

"When you die," I say, "you're supposed to run toward the white light."

"What white light?"

"I've just heard about it," I say.

"I won't be doing any running, honey."

"This is after you drop the body, Dad," I say. "Your soul can run toward the white light or take rebirth, distracted by all sorts of possibilities."

"Maybe I could come back as a better father."

"You did the best you could," I say. "You did fine."

"I did the best I could." He looks doubtful.

"I know you did."

"You do?" he says. "I did?"

10

Trust Issues

Once I dated a cowboy, when I first came to Texas. He drove over to my apartment building, parked in front, raised the hood of his pickup, and started working on the engine. He never called to say he was coming or knocked to say he was there. If I didn't want to see him, I wasn't supposed to go out, and if I did want to see him, I was. After a while, I brought him out a beer.

I long for that kind of simplicity with Gabriel. But he and I belong to another world—of self-defense and networking, of homelessness and divorce.

"We've got to talk," Gabriel says when I walk in from the airport.

I follow him into the kitchen, where he's making pancakes and smoothies. We must have had our nanosecond, and I was in Boston and missed it. I pick up the measuring cup and mix. I'll get the measuring cup if he asks me to move out, but the mix is his.

"Sorry I got sideways with you," he says, and tests the griddle. Two drops of water sizzle and steam.

"About my family?"

"About my mother," he says. "But I figured out why you won't take me to meet your folks."

Just as I'm about to tell him I tried to call him to explain, the phone on the kitchen counter rings. He answers it, then goes to the bedroom phone and shuts the door.

A woman's voice comes through the receiver lying on the counter, like alarming signals from outer space. I hang up the phone and pour pancake mix and water into the mixing bowl without reading the directions.

"I put too much water in the mix," I say when Gabriel comes back.

He reads the directions. "Equal amounts of mix and water," he says, and dumps two more cups of mix into the bowl. "There'll be pancakes left over for some other time."

"For you and your other girlfriend?" I wouldn't want to eat pancakes he made with someone else.

"What other girlfriend?"

"The one on the phone."

"My ex-wife?"

"Sorry," I say. "What can we do with our leftover pancakes?"

He hands me the blender. "You be in charge of our smoothies."

It's not hard to trust someone you hardly know, because all you're trusting is who you think he is. On the other hand, you can trust someone you've been through a lot of crises with. Gabriel and I are stuck in the middle, lost between these two. We know each other well enough to have had our projections destroyed, but we haven't survived our first crisis yet.

"I'm a bull in the china shop of divorce," I say. I break eggs and slice bananas into the blender.

"A calf, maybe," he says.

I turn on the blender. Raw egg and bananas run out the bottom all over the kitchen counter and onto the floor. "It's hopeless," I say.

"This is a left-hand screw," he says. "Most blenders screw onto the base to the right."

"How many blenders have you had?"

"This is my first since my divorce. Felicity got the other one." He takes a sponge and helps me wipe up the mess I've made of our smoothies, until we both smell the pancakes burning. He lunges for the spatula.

"I don't know why I bungle so much in your kitchen," I say. "I was fine in my own."

We sit on the balcony and eat our burnt pancakes. The air is cool after a brief shower. There's a rainbow over the Summit, just as there was the evening the Rockets won their first NBA championship. Maybe he'll never be able to ask me to move out and I'll just live with him forever.

"There's no one else," Gabriel says, after a while.

"I have some trust issues," I say. I pour maple syrup over the rubbery pancakes to break them down.

"Have some myself," he says. "I work all day in the E.R. with people in terrible shape, but when it comes to listening to Felicity I'm a basket case."

"She's a walking emergency."

"I'm trying to take responsibility for my part in our divorce," he says, "without taking all the blame."

"Why can't you say it's all her fault?"

"That's the temptation." He attacks his stack of pancakes. "If I make her out to be a witch, then I won't learn what I need to about myself to keep it from happening again."

"I have to learn what it was about Web that connected with something in myself."

"I struggle with my inner witch; you struggle with your trickster," he says, in the nouveau-Jungian terms of the men's movement.

"Why can't our archetypes be friends?" I have to give Gabriel credit for trying to balance his masculine and feminine energies.

"Today in the E.R I had a battered husband," he says. "He's divorced from his wife but they live in the same house."

"What marital status did he put on his medical record?"

"It was blank so I wrote in 'pissed off,'" he says.

"Did you work in the E.R the whole time I was in Boston?"

"On my day off I wrote a paper on burnout for the *New England Journal of Medicine*, " he says.

"You burned out writing a paper on burnout."

"I'm burning, but not out," he says.

"How do you stand the misery of emergency medicine?"

"I like the urgency," he says. "It's like being a fireman— the bell rings and you go."

"Doesn't anything happy happen in the E.R?"

"Not really." He flips through a sports equipment catalog from the stack under his chair. Sometimes when he can't sleep, he gets up and reads catalogs on the balcony by flashlight.

"Do you buy things from your catalogs?" I say.

"No," he says. "I read them to take my mind off things."

"Like what, right now?"

"Off the gunshot victim I treated today, whose wife put out a contract on him through her hairdresser."

He looks intently at me for a long time. Life with Gabriel is like living hopefully in the dark night of the soul. I thought I could be surprised by happiness if I were in the right place at the right time. I'd be properly positioned, as the women in my networking group say.

"Let's go for a drive," he says.

We leave the dishes, go down to the parking lot, climb into his truck. We open the pickup windows to the balmy Texas breeze. I'm shocked to find I love a city I didn't expect to even like. The downtown skyline glows to the east, the Galleria skyline to the west. In between, we cruise long stretches of softly lighted houses, wide bay windows framing families watching TV.

"Whenever I'm happy," I say, "I feel guilty about the people who aren't."

Gabriel moves my hand over to his thigh, puts his hand over mine. "Our cup is half full," he says.

"But half the world's cup is empty," I say.

We pass blocks of outdoor discos, and Mexican and seafood restaurants, people sipping margaritas out on the decks. The night streams by like a carnival seen from a merry-go-round—red, blue, neon.

We stop at the Transco Tower, tapering upward sixty-four stories. Its reflective glass mirrors the city back to itself. The rotating beacon on top searches the skies. What's it searching for? We walk the grassy three acres beneath it, toward the Transco Fountain. During the day, families picnic in the green park, children roll down the sloping sides. Everyone comes here, from River Oaks and Montrose and the barrios. At dusk, lovers lie in the sweet-smelling grass, pull each other close. This late, only a few couples are left in the moist darkness.

"Do you hear bells?" I ask Gabriel. The night is full of ringing, as of hundreds of tambourines.

"Those are Texan crickets," he says.

We walk up the steps and through the middle of the three

arches in front of the fountain. Alone, we stare at the curved wall of cascading water, sixty-four feet high. Soon the water and the white light behind it will be turned off for the night.

Gabriel turns to speak to me. His eyes, deep with love, meet mine. "Will you marry me?" he says, in the roar of the waterfall.

I know I want to marry Gabriel when I realize that something as intimate as my own anxiety can make me unhappy no longer. "Yes," I whisper. Love rushes through me, over me.

"Beg pardon?" He looks at me through the steamy mist.

"Yes," I say, above the roar this time.

He takes a small black velvet box from his pocket and pries open the lid. The diamond blazes with light, deep in its setting, like the single star piercing the sky above us.

With shocking suddenness, the waterfall turns off for the night. Gabriel and I stand in the total darkness, silent except for the echo bouncing off the colossal stone wall: Yes! Yes! Yes!

He takes the ring from its velvet, slides it onto my finger. I sway with love. We hold onto each other. We kiss as we never have before, wave upon wave of desire and relief. "I love you," we whisper, even our whispers echoing back and forth on the high empty wall.

We walk back out through the middle arch we came in, down the steps. A homeless man steps out of the shadows. He stops a few feet from us, almost politely, as if not to scare us. Gabriel reaches into his pocket and hands him some bills. The man mutters gratefully.

"I figured out you wouldn't take me to meet your family long as we just lived together," he says. "I would've asked you to marry me before, but I wasn't sure you'd say yes. Wasn't sure this evening, but it was a chance I had to take."

How could I have read him so wrong?

I take his hand. We walk toward the truck.

"The diamond is beautiful," I say. I look down at my hand as if seeing it for the first time. It's a Texas-sized diamond, in a classic, six-prong platinum Tiffany setting.

"Did I get the right one?" he says.

"Yes," I say. "You did."

Making love with Gabriel reminds me of learning to dive. I was at Girl Scout camp, on a cool lake murky with a sandy bottom. Further out on the dock, the older girls dove gracefully, while close to shore, the Brownies practiced their dog paddles. In between, my swimming class lined up on our part of the wooden dock, the palms of our hands together in prayer position, arms raised over our lean bodies. Curling their toes on the edge, a few learned quickly how to arc into the breast-deep water. Others followed, then clambered back onto the dock in their wet swimsuits to dive again.

At first, I couldn't allow myself to do it. Our instructor reasoned with me, but it was not a fear to be reasoned with. My body would not obey. What was it that kept me from arcing? Having failed to push off, my shins crashed on the edge of the dock as I belly-flopped onto the water.

Gabriel's hands grow large with tenderness; his fingertips brush my breasts. We slow down, weighted with desire. We swim down together to the cool sheet. We signal like divers, swimming down, into our subterranean garden. I'm caught in the seaweed of his legs, he in the seaweed of my hair. We tumble, scud along the bottom.

A sea anemone opens, too slowly for the naked eye. He makes love to me until my mind loses its grip on its fear, renunciation. I dive and dive; he dives with me.

We hurtle forward at the shocking speed of light.

11

Self-Destruct Instructor

Does driving in rush hour make us so driven? Speeding up since the eighties' influx of Yankees, Houston speech has reached a feverish pitch in the traffic reports. The radio stations put drumbeat soundtracks behind the hysterical voices of the announcers, broadcasting live from helicopters buzzing over us. All around me, men talk on car phones, women put on makeup. Pickups get off the freeway whenever they feel like it, barrel down the steep slopes between exits, leave wide muddy tracks in the grass.

I hold the city in my mind, try to visualize my way around the traffic jams—an overturned eighteen-wheeler where the Southwest Freeway careens into the Loop, massive construction on the Gulf Freeway, a dazed cow loose on 288. I inch forward so I won't get bumped from behind. If I am, I'll have only seconds to decide whether I'm being carjacked.

My hand on the steering wheel, my diamond ring flashes in the morning Texas sun. I've passed over from a have-not to a have, at once exultant and guilty.

Unable to wait until our self-defense class this evening to tell Gigi I'm engaged, I call her from my cellular phone. She's not at home, in her office, or her car, so her secretary patches me through to her.

"I said yes to Gabriel in the nanosecond," I say when I reach her at a breakfast meeting.

"You'll have to start using hairspray."

"I'm not making the commitment to my hair."

"Gabriel won't want a wife with wild hair," she says. "The point of hairspray is your hair settles down."

"It moves anyway," I say. "Then my hair is stuck out of place."

"You're making it more complicated than it is," she says.

I compartmentalize my life by my phone lines—Gabriel and Gigi on my cellular phone, Chance on my library line. Web doesn't fit in anymore, but that doesn't stop him.

"How did you get past Lucille?" I demand when he reaches me at the library. I told Lucille not to put Web through anymore. She hates me, but not that much.

"I told her I was Gabriel," he says.

I gasp in exasperation.

"I had a good reason," he says. "A dance contest in Cozumel."

"I'm engaged to be married."

"This isn't a bachelor party," he says.

It's not that I'm such a great dancer, Web's a terrific lead. He'd whirl me around the dance floor in the tango, the meringue, the music flowing electrically through his wrist to mine. Men like Web who are too good at one thing don't feel they have to be good at anything else.

"You have plenty of other partners," I say.

"You're the best," he says. "Besides, you don't want to marry a guy like that."

Slim and wiry, he was born to wear a tux and cummerbund. Muscular men like Gabriel seem always about to split something, no matter how elegant their tailoring.

"You've never met him."

"I can picture the kind of guy you'd get messed up when I'm not there."

"At least he's not a polygamist."

"I have the polygamy hormone."

"There's no such thing."

"They've studied it in ducks," he says. "Polygamy is the answer to my emotional, financial, and spiritual problems."

I feel as guilty talking to Web as if I were having phone sex. If Web were always appalling, it'd be easier to forget him. But they're never all bad—Web, my father, Chance. I mistrust them for simple reasons and like them for complicated ones.

"Anyway, you'd like me better now," he goes on. "I'm in group therapy."

"On the ship?"

"It's the favorite activity."

"How many women in the group are you dating?"

"Just a few," he says. "I'm trying to find a good relationship."

"Good," I say. "As long as it's not with me."

With Web I was psychosexually homeless, begging for crumbs from the table of his promiscuity. "Goodbye," I say. "I have to go take library service to the homeless."

"America's melting pot melted too much," he says. "It's a meltdown."

The harder I work on my homeless report, the more unwieldy it becomes.

Vanessa pokes her head into my office to read my laptop

screen over my shoulder. "A groundbreaking homeless proposal would revolutionize library service," she says. "But
this isn't it."

I'm relieved when Chance calls and takes me away from
my desk. I meet him at a Stop N Go.

"You moving in the right direction," he says when I tell
him I'm engaged. "But I know you going to relapse."

"Gabriel and I love each other."

"That don't mean nothing, push come to shove," he says.
"What's he like?"

"He's an emergency room doctor," I say, "from a wealthy
Fort Worth family with a ranch. He has a two-year-old son
from his first marriage."

"Sounds like trouble all the way around."

"Don't you believe I can have a successful relationship
and get married?" I say. "I believe you can get a job and have
the life you want."

"No you don't."

"You'll see," I say. "I'll send you an invitation to my wedding, and you'll be able to come."

"They won't let me in, looking like I do."

Is he growing more gaunt from drugs, or hunger? In any
case, he has a contact at a battered women's shelter and
wants me to talk to the homeless women there.

"Aren't most battered women's shelters' addresses
secret?" I say.

He fidgets for a moment. "I been through their program
for batterers," he says. He searches my eyes.

"Did you try to get along with your wife?"

"Me, I mean, for real, I guess, I tell people she's my wife,
we go out together, I don't overcrowd her, don't get too
cocky, I'm real gentle, flow, you let yourself flow," he says.
"When she flow, that make them other nuts go crazy, and

that make them think they can come in and mess up a relationship. But when both of y'all are bonded as one, why should I worry? This is what I went through, but my thoughts went—that way." He points his two index fingers in opposite directions.

A police car siren screams by. How many nights did my brother and I watch wide-eyed while a policeman took away our father, an ambulance took away our mother?

"And my thoughts went that way because she let me down," he goes on. "I had believed in my support being strong. You pulling one way and the other one's pulling the other, it's hard to make it."

Will Gabriel and I pull the same way? A neighbor would finally arrive to comfort my brother and me—with a cookie, a soft drink.

"Let's get you something to eat," I say to Chance.

First he calls the battered women's shelter on the store's pay phone. He talks to someone there to get me a kind of security clearance. On Chance's recommendation I'm given directions, while he buys a hot dog, microwaves it, covers it with ketchup and mustard to balance his diet.

He's outside eating when I come back to my car. A mangy white dog limps up and gives him a plaintive look. Chance gives him half his hot dog. The dog wags his tail.

The shelter is in a poor neighborhood on the fringes of downtown. It crouches in the shadow of the freeway, while the world rushes by on the overpass. Women peer out through the burglar bars on the shelter's windows. They eye me suspiciously when I knock on the heavy door.

In the waiting room they wait, at this urgent moment in their lives, to see a counselor, to get busfare to a social service office. I waited with my mother, before there were women's shelters. She took my brother and me with her to the doctor's, when she was pregnant with our new baby. We waited with her at the courthouse, where she was trying to get someone to undo the rule that said we had to live with Dad. We sat with her on a bench, Dougie leaning against one side of her and I against her other. At the doctor's office she clutched her small warm jar of urine, but at the courthouse held nothing in her fingers, slim and trembling. These became confused in my mind, because she came to the doctor's and the courthouse as a supplicant, pleading quietly with strange men. All the men behind the doors became the one man—doctor, judge, priest, landlord—who would legislate the life of our new baby, our safety and our salvation and our poverty, while we sat in waiting room after waiting room. Our baby came and went back again to God, as softly as a ghost.

I twist the band of my engagement ring around and around on my finger. Sandra, the young woman who has volunteered to talk with me, trudges into the shelter's waiting room. I stand to say hello; she gives me a pinched smile. Dark circles are purple under her eyes.

"Can you read, Sandra?" I ask her. We sit down side by side on folding chairs.

"If I could read better, it might help me find a job," she says. "I've been working out of the labor pool; it's nice, you get paid the same day. If you work real good, and the supervisor sees that, you might get a permanent job. I've done cleaning at offices, put tags on clothes at a store to get ready for a big sale."

"How old are your kids?"

"My oldest daughter's six, my son is five, my daughter after him is three, the baby just turned one," she says. "I'm saving the money I make while I'm here so I can get my children some clothes. The one thing I need is a job, and that you have to go out and get on your own." She says this as if she has been told it many times.

"What kind of work are you interested in?" I say.

"Right now, I'm interested in doing some cleaning," she says. "I've been to school, but basically I'm just trying to get some things straightened out. I still have stuff I need to move out of the church cafeteria. Since we can't go home because my husband's still there, I got to get my records transferred. I got a lot of business to take care of. It's a help, but it causes a lot of problems too, because you got to go when they tell you, you may be on a job and you just got off the day before. It's too many stipulations. Then when you get a job, they cut you back on your check, and you ain't making that much anyway. I like the help, I'm not complaining, it's just I don't like all this getting off from work and coming and going. With the children it gets hectic."

"Have you had a steady job in the past?"

"I did work, off and on, but I didn't keep anything steady," she says. "Nursing homes, I've had several jobs. Whenever things got too hard for me to handle, I'd run. Live somewhere else and try to make it. But you have to start over wherever you go. I'm looking for an apartment. I'm hoping it'll be cheap rent, but I don't mind paying, it depends on where it is. If you're living in a depressing area, it makes you not want to pay much rent. I hope there's somewhere I won't have to move from for a while. I'm really, really tired."

"What are your long-term goals?"

"I don't plan on messing up until I get what I came here for," she says. "Stability, really, and to be settled. First time I left my husband, I was trying to do everything myself, but it was like confusing. I was out in the world and it swallowed me up; I couldn't get no direction. Here, with the curfew, you have to be in at eight and you can either sit and look stupid or plan what you're going to do the next day. It's like a way to discipline yourself."

"Is that difficult?" I say.

"It's not like you walk around ashamed, because you know that everybody here has some kind of problem," she says. "It's not like you're better than I am, or I'm better than you. Just think, if we weren't here, where would we be?"

After the courthouse, after the doctor's, our mother took us to the five and ten. She'd lift first Dougie, then me, up to the toy counter to choose a small package of colored clay, or a tiny metal circus with a magnetic clown, or a folded model airplane made of wood as thin as paper. Our sorrow was tainted with the exquisite wonder of small pleasures, our delight tainted with sorrow, like the different colors of streaked clay, blue and yellow as we rolled it into snakes and balls.

After we lost our baby and Dad left, Mother and Dougie and I went to live in the project. In the project, the other mothers grew fat and strident, while ours grew thinner and more quiet. At suppertime, the mothers hung out their back doors and yelled for their kids—*Juuunior, Bawwwbby, Anthonyyyyy.* Especially in the summer, when the kids played as far as the dump, the mothers took deep breaths and sang out the names of their children. Dougie and I went home without being called; we could feel our mother worrying about us. We went in and washed our hands, sat down with her at the small Formica dinette.

For supper we might each have a hot dog, rolled up in Wonder Bread. What was it like for my mother to have only her children for company, and to eat children's food? But we didn't feel poor; we weren't poor, we were afraid. Fear was our poverty. Dougie and I shared the overwhelming longing to comfort Mother, to say something or do something or to be the kind of child who once and for all could make her worry go away, and ours with it. "Is Daddy still mad at us?" I asked. "Will he follow us here?" My mother stopped answering me; that was the beginning of her silence. At first, she seemed not to answer because she was busy worrying it out, chewing her lower lip, nibbling at her nails. I'd give her time to worry, and ask her again. But her fear turned to anger, as if I created the problem by asking the question.

I say goodbye to Sandra, and take sidestreets home instead of the freeway. I cherish the moment at an intersection when the traffic is stopped in all four directions. I forget I'm waiting for the light to change. Stillness descends on me, a weird kind of blessing.

My bruises barely have time to fade before I acquire a new set in each self-defense class. I now think of Bubba as my self-destruct instructor.

Gigi's eyes fall on my ring when I walk into the Women's Center. "That's no diamond," she says. "It's the Transco Tower beacon."

Susan, Marcy, and Barbara crowd around to congratulate me.

"All right, girls," Bubba says. "Let's get started. Colleen first, on account of a mugger'd love to get that ring."

"You'll flunk self-defense if you refuse to use the hand your ring is on," Gigi says, after I've failed my turn.

"It doesn't seem right to punch someone with Gabriel's ring," I say.

"How'd you ever get him to propose?" she says.

"He wants to meet my family," I say. "He no longer

wants to compromise my honor by just living together."

"He's a man of the nineties—the eighteen nineties," she says "Are you ready to get married?"

"Ready as I *can* be," I say. "But is Gabriel?"

"That's a question you can't afford to ask," she says. "He'll get over his divorce when you're not looking and someone else will get him."

In any case, I don't have to use my engaged hand to punch today, because we have to learn to kick lying down. We spread out gym mats to fall on. Bubba knocks us down in turn, shows us how to fall, kick, knock him backwards.

"My heart isn't in this," I tell Gigi. "I hate living in a world so violent I have to learn violence to defend myself."

"What about the power imbalances in your relationship with Gabriel?" she says. "What about Prince Charles and Princess Di?"

"He makes more money. It's his apartment. He's the one who gets to propose," I say. "Do you think he'll stifle me?"

"You need someone to stifle you," she says.

"At least he's not a misogynist."

"All men are misogynists," she says.

"How's it going with you and Malcolm?"

"My love-life has been reduced to emoticons," she says, referring to the graphic symbols for computer feelings.

Halfway through his ground attack on Susan, Bubba jumps up. "What'd she do wrong?" he says.

None of us know.

"She turned away," he says, "and brought joy to my rapist's heart. Never turn your back on your attacker; never turn the other cheek. Jesus did that, but we ain't that good."

"That's not what Jesus meant," Marcy says.

Bubba declines this opportunity for a theological discussion. He introduces the element of surprise, attacks us randomly instead of in turn. "On the street, you're going to have more fear," he says. "You'll create it—you create fear." He makes it sound as if fear, perhaps anything, is something we actually *make*.

"What about all your fears?" Gigi asks me. "Of Gabriel meeting your father, of intimacy and marriage?"

"I had them organized in my mind," I say, "but when he proposed I forgot them."

"What will you do when they come back?"

"Right now I'm just feeling what it's like to be engaged," I say. At the women's college I went to, the other girls got engaged over and over to every man they slept with.

"Don't get married just to feel what that's like," she says.

"We won't do it until next spring, at the earliest," I say.

"Do it before he changes his mind."

Bubba paces back and forth in front of us, biding his time.

"Web called to beg me to be his partner at a dance contest in Cozumel," I say to Gigi.

"Make Gabriel take you dancing."

"He hates to dance," I say. "And when would we find the time? He has to rearrange his call schedule to make love to me."

Gigi frowns; Marcy, Susan, and Barbara exchange looks.

"What if the attacker takes me by surprise when I'm asleep?" I ask Bubba. Gabriel often works all night in the E.R.

"Worst possible scenario," Bubba says, and stops in his tracks. "Here's this guy, middle of the night. Just you and him."

We spring into our curled positions on our mats, poised to kick.

"Lie flat on your back, arms up like this," he says to me.

I uncurl, flop back on the mat.

He crouches over me. "Go for my eyes," he says. He shows me how to bunch my fingers and jab.

"Yuck," I say.

"Yuck?" he says. "The attacker could have one eye hangin' outta his socket. That don't matter."

I go for his eyes, then try to flip him, but I flip him the wrong way, on top of me.

"You lose," he says. "You got to flip him fast and in the right direction. It's like bulldoggin' cattle."

"Send Gabriel to Victoria's Secret to buy you some sexy lingerie," Gigi says as I stagger up. "That should help your body make peace with your mind."

"What if he falls in love with the saleswoman?" I say.

"What if our mugger has a gun?" Barbara asks Bubba.

"That's a different level," he says. "Y'all are in mugger kindergarten."

"It's a good thing you're living with Gabriel before you marry him," Gigi tells me, "so you have to deal with only one level of the I-We crisis at a time."

12

That's What a Maid of Honor Is For

My engagement to Gabriel shifts the power balance in my friendship with Gigi. She has always bossed me around a little, but I trusted her to boss me around in the right direction. We're at the same achievement level in our careers, but now I've pulled out ahead in the marriage category. I defuse the potential conflict in the only way that comes to mind. "Gigi," I say when I call her. "Will you be my maid of honor? The wedding will be in early spring."

For a minute she's speechless. "Okay," she says. "But you'll have to do everything I tell you."

I'd remind her I'm the bride, but I don't want to rub it in. "I'll take it under advisement," I say, like Vanessa when she means to disregard everything I say.

"Your first step is the first toward any goal," she says. "Shopping."

"How many steps are there?"

"Twelve, like with everything," she says. "The first ten are shopping, and the eleventh is the wedding."

"What's the twelfth?"

"Exchanging."

"Rings?"

"Gifts," she says. "You're going to get too much of some things and not enough of others, just like in your relationship. At least with shopping, you get a chance to right the balance."

When she comes over to pick me up to go shopping at the Galleria, I show her the designer dresses, hats, purses, and shoes that Peaches sent me from the Fort Worth Neiman Marcus. Expensive clothes like these fit perfectly, in my size or not.

"Peaches is so good to me," I say.

"Either she likes you," Gigi says, "or she's appalled by your style."

"How would you describe my style?"

"Defiantly trendy," she says.

"Do you think she thinks I'm good enough for Gabriel?" I say. "She knows I grew up in a housing project."

"Yes, but you have beautiful manners and a superb education."

"I was quality poor," I say. "When I marry Gabriel, will I be quality rich like him and his parents?"

"What matters is you love Gabriel," she says.

Gigi and I go to the Galleria in Gigi's BMW because her trunk is bigger than mine. She gives new meaning to the phrase *trunk show*. She's a Preferred Customer everywhere. She shops for sport, not need.

We park on Level Two in the middle part of the Galleria. Gigi likes to position her car centrally so she can return and lock packages inside it. She keeps her arms free to grab things off racks, dab on sample perfumes, try on jewelry, shoes, cosmetics.

"I hate shopping," I say. My mother and I used to shop with our hearts in our mouths, and only for something we'd needed for a long time. We'd go from store to store, trying to find the right size or the right color for some price we could barely afford. "Do I really like it?" my mother would ask me for days afterward. We couldn't afford to make a mistake.

"If I don't hate it, I buy it," Gigi says. "Do you realize people come from all over the world just to shop at our Galleria?"

"Because the dollar's dropping," I say.

But the dollar's not dropping for her. She floats through the Galleria as lightly as the ice-skaters on the rink in the middle. We hang over the railing to watch them. I look at the levels above and below us, ringed with as many miles of shops as this one. The Galleria has three levels—heaven, purgatory, and hell.

"What kind of bridal gown do you want?" Gigi says. "What's your china pattern, your flatware, your crystal?"

"I've never thought about it."

"Don't you read the magazines?"

"I read *Library Journal*," I say. *"The New Yorker, People, Vegetarian Times."*

"Even they have advertising."

"I never thought I'd get married."

The first frothy white wedding gown I try on has a tiny waist, antebellum skirt, off-the-shoulder puff sleeves. "I love it," I say.

"Too much cleavage," Gigi says. "Gabriel might think you're up to something."

"What could I possibly be up to on my wedding day?"

"I just want to get you married off," she says. "After that, you're Gabriel's problem."

The saleswoman whisks away that dress as soon as I've stepped out of it. I try on several others, then I start to look at the price tags. "Ten thousand dollars!" I say. "I can't spend that kind of money on a dress for one day."

"Everyone has to spend at least two thousand," Gigi says. "It's a symptom of self-esteem."

"Fifteen dollars will provide meals for eleven homeless people," I say. "Fifty-one will provide meals for thirty-seven, and one hundred and two for seventy-four homeless people. How many people could eat for a two-thousand-dollar wedding gown?"

"Only you would turn looking for a wedding gown into a personal moral crisis about the homeless."

"I refuse to get my marriage to Gabriel off on the wrong karmic foot," I say, and stamp mine.

Gigi looks down at my feet. "Wait 'til you see how much white satin bridal pumps cost."

The saleswoman gapes at us. A gown hangs over her arm like a fainted bride.

"Let's move on, we can't burn out at ten-thirty in the morning on the bridal gown," Gigi says. "We have to pace ourselves. Shopping for a wedding takes months, sometimes years." Her dark eyes shine.

I sway with dizzy apprehension. Actually, I'm glad Gigi is making me shop because I'd never shop alone. The loneliness of it, the heavy weight of objects, things, stuff that draws away human energy. The stores glare with fluorescence, light so false you can't tell what color anything really is. The air is stuffy with fallout from synthetic textiles, polluting the air like fake pollen. At malls, all the stores open on one side to possess you before you consent, to draw you in before you can ritualistically open a door and prepare yourself. The clerks bog down frantically in their endless payment procedures, checking identification, ringing up the sales, removing shoplifting tags, wrapping things in cumbersome bags. Everything slows to an inertia that makes the customers line up crazy with hurry, so they can go on to the next errand to reenact the consumer psychodrama all over again.

"What you need is a good strong cup of French roast and a chocolate croissant," Gigi says.

"You're right about the croissant," I say, "but you know how I get with coffee."

She drags me off to one of those coffee shoppes where the coffee costs four dollars a cup and a tiny pastry is three dollars. "See," she says, "the dollar's not down." She orders cappuccino for both of us. They grind the beans.

I never drink coffee; I save it to use as a drug because it makes me ecstatic. In about five minutes I won't be able to stop talking; I'll be confessing all sorts of things to Gigi. "You're trying to make me buy things," I say.

"You need everything," she says. "Not just china and crystal, but monogrammed linens, stationery, luggage, your trousseau, satin clothes hangers; you need—"

"Gigi, please. I need to lie down, the coffee's hitting."

"You act like someone who lives where you can't even *get* cappuccino—Alabama or someplace."

"You can get cappuccino in Alabama. But you don't just get crystal and china. You have to deserve it."

"What, do you think you can get everything overnight, as much as you need?" she says. She had a big wedding with lots of presents, followed by a big divorce with lots of acrimony.

"Where's your silver now?" I ask her.

"In the vault."

"You have a vault?"

"Actually, it's a mini-warehouse," she says.

I study her while she eats the froth in the bottom of her cup with a tiny spoon. "What did you like about Henry?"

"He gave good wallet," she says.

"Where is he now?"

"Somewhere boring," she says. "Not Cozumel, like Web."

"What worries me about Web is he's moving closer, like a hurricane," I say. "I felt safer when he was in Aruba. What if he sails from the Caribbean into the Gulf of Mexico?"

"Board up your windows," she says. "Married women are his favorite, but engaged, you're a close second."

To distract myself from the picture of Web whipping tropical romances into Category Three storms, I focus on autumn in the Galleria. People create autumn in Houston by turning their air conditioners to cold, so they can wear their fall clothes. Gigi wears a red cashmere turtleneck.

"Is that a new turtleneck?" I say.

"Nothing on me is new," she says. "Everything is used."

"But you're always buying new outfits."

"I have a great new clingy sweater-dress," she says, "but I refuse to wear it until someone asks me out who's worthy of it."

"Let's go on to the second step of shopping," I say. I treat for the cappuccino and pastry. Gigi's so sure shopping is emotionally stabilizing, I want to believe it too.

We rush off to the china department at Tiffany—walls and walls of five-piece place settings.

"Two hundred dollars for a dinner plate!" I say, and pick up one with blue frogs doing a minuet in a rose garden.

"You don't have to get sixteen place settings today," Gigi says. "You just have to start thinking about your pattern."

"My pattern is failure."

"Who makes it?" the bridal registry consultant asks.

"I inherited it."

She sets up the long mahogany display table with lace place mats and china. "You need to choose patterns that work together," she says.

"How?" I say. "Each one speaks to a different part of my personality. They make me feel conflicted."

"Choose the one that's the real you," Gigi says.

"Do you have something spiritual?" I say to the consultant, who looks at me oddly. "I'm a spiritual wannabe."

"I'm sorry I made you drink the coffee, Colleen," Gigi says. "You're too ecstatic already."

"That white plate with the royal blue rim speaks to the registered voter in me," I say, "but it'd be too much like eating at an insurance banquet. The one with the green and yellow fleurs-de-lis reminds me of Girl Scouts. This pink and white garland speaks of my daughterly piety but no man would ever eat off of it. My favorite so far is this one with the butterflies freaking out over the red and blue flowers." I sit down in front of it and imagine dinner with Gabriel. Would my Vegetables Pernod look good on it?

"You might consider a simple pattern in your flatware if you choose that china," the consultant says.

"Not too simple," I say. "My everyday flatware is Stolen Dormitory."

She sets up twelve five-piece place settings of the china I kind of like, with twelve different silver patterns—knife, dinner fork, salad fork, teaspoon, soup spoon, fish knife, butter knife, demitasse spoon for each. I play musical chairs with myself, stay put at one that reminds me of Versailles.

The consultant clears the table of all the other silver and sets up eleven other place settings of my favorite, then brings out twelve different patterns of crystal. Goblets, glasses for red wine and white wine, hock and cordial glasses, champagne flutes and champagne-sherbets. Tumblers and highball glasses and glasses for drinks you'd have to go to bartending school to find out about.

I pick up a silver pie-server and stare into it, try to see my real self. "Gigi," I say. "I can't afford this stuff."

"You don't *buy* it," she says. "When you get married people give you everything."

If I don't get china, I don't get Gabriel. I'll move back to my old apartment in the Lord's Motel, grow old eating off of a plastic tray and drinking from a plastic cup with one of those bent straws. "I'll take that china, that crystal, that flatware," I say.

"We'll come back to register later," Gigi says to the consultant. "I have to make sure it isn't the caffeine."

I tear myself away from all my patterns. I already see Gabriel at one end of the dining room table, carving our vegetarian turkey.

"Let's go watch the ice-skaters," I say.

Gay men in Armani suits tear past us, toting Tiffany shopping bags.

"At least Gabriel isn't gay," Gigi says. "Although it'd be better to love a gay man than a closety straight one."

"He's not gay, but he's not homophobic either."

"Thank God," she says. "One day all the men turned wimpy; now even the straight men are gay. There are a few married men you can be sort of tentatively affectionate with if you're friends with their wives. Most of the divorced men are still in love with their ex's, and they like you if you're a little redhead with a mole behind your left earlobe like hers. Then there are the engineers in gold Porsches who take you out for nice dinners but can't talk about anything. You're lucky you've found a man who's not denatured."

"Vanessa says the women's movement denatured the men," I say. "But why didn't those men keep up with the women's movement through the men's movement?"

"Some of them did; they're all married and can cook," she says. "Anyway, the biggest difference between sexual preferences is not between straight and gay, but between with yourself and with others."

The music stops and the skaters clear the ice for the machine that smooths it after they've hacked it all to bits. I gaze down on it and hope Gabriel is having a good day in the E.R.

"It's a long way from the Galleria to the altar," I say.

"Your coffee has worn off," she says. "Let's go have lunch at a crêperie. This is the biggest shopping project you'll ever undertake."

"I'll need an undertaker before its over," I say.

"I'll help you through it," she says. "That's what a maid of honor is for."

13

If Lost, Relax

"Dad really had to try to screw up so well!" my brother Doug calls to tell me. "As legatee of that dead woman's estate he's liable for estate and property taxes, not to mention utility and other bills."

"We have to do something," I say.

"Her relatives are suing him," he goes on. "The day before Thanksgiving he has to appear in probate court, to try to get clear title to the house she supposedly left him."

"But he's sick," I say.

"He's broke!"

Gabriel is grieving over not having visitation with Gabe this Thanksgiving. With dread I invite him to come home to Boston with me. He's determined to meet my family now that we're engaged. I just hope it doesn't make him change his mind.

My father had visitation with Doug and me every Thanksgiving, as long as he came to us in the housing project. Sometimes he showed up drunk, sometimes sober, sometimes not at all.

On the Wednesday morning before Thanksgiving, we

can't find a parking place at Houston Intercontinental Airport. The expensive short-term garage and the outlying long-term parking lots are all full.

"We're going to miss our flight," I say. We've driven in circles for an hour.

"You go check in," Gabriel says. He drops me off with our bags. "I'll think of something."

I wait at the gate while everyone else boards. Is this what it would be like to wait at the altar? I asked my mother once how my father handled a crisis. "He always said he'd take care of it," she said. "But he never did."

Gabriel races up seconds before they close the door to the airplane.

"Where did you park?" I say.

"Five miles away," he says, out of breath. "I had to run to the airport because there wasn't a shuttle."

"That's why I'm marrying you," I say.

We hold hands during take-off, then I pull my pocket survival guide out of my purse. The plastic card tells in microscopic print which berries and grasses are edible, and how to build an igloo, treat snakebite, get water from a cactus, signal from the ground you need guns and ammo. It says you can tell you're exhausted if the sky is receding. I look out the window. The sky is receding, but it should be if you're in it.

"'If Lost, Relax'?" Gabriel says, reading the card's first line.

"I'll need this if the plane crashes," I say. "I didn't go to National Outdoor Leadership School like you."

"If it crashes, stick with me." He puts his arm around me, holds me as close as the armrest between us will allow.

"My father's still homeless," I say, over the roar of the airplane.

"Harmless?"

"I wish. Homeless. Homeless."

He looks as if the plane just crashed. "Did you tell him we're engaged?"

"Not yet." I don't want my father to put a hex on it. "You can tell him when you meet him."

He's still in shock when we take a taxi from Boston's Logan Airport to my mother's house. At least I'm not bringing Gabriel home to a housing project.

My mother is bending over in her driveway, watching a beetle.

"Hi, Mom," I say. "This is Gabriel."

"Hello, Gabriel," she says, and looks through him with her pale blue eyes. She knows we're engaged, but is reserving judgment until she sees what a Texan is like. She's the opposite of Gabriel's mother—Peaches is all over you like a puppy, while my mother is reserved like a cat.

"Pleased to meet you," Gabriel says. He looks relieved she isn't homeless.

"What are you doing?" I ask her.

"This beetle has been on his back all morning so I finally decided to come out and turn him right-side up," she says.

The beetle is large and brown. He takes a few steps, then falls over on his back again.

Gabriel, my mother, and I take a few turns at turning him right-side up, but he refuses to stay that way. We do it one last time, then go into the house without looking back.

Gabriel insists on accompanying me to my father's hearing in probate court. We borrow my mother's car to pick up my father at the veterans' convalescent home he's been in since he got out of the hospital.

"I hope we meet again under better circumstances," my father says to Gabriel as we help him into the car. He wheezes, his jowls riding up and down.

"Just don't die until we get this resolved," I say.

"This feels like the Last Judgment, honey," he says. He wears his one tweed sportcoat, baggy pants, threadbare shirt.

"Think of it as a dress rehearsal," I say.

Gabriel drops off my father and me at the courthouse door, then goes to park the car. My father walks so slowly that Gabriel catches up with us before we enter the courtroom. The three of us sit down near the front, my father between Gabriel and me.

The courtroom feels cold, as if they've already turned off the heat for the holiday weekend. It's decorated for Thanksgiving; festoons of orange, brown, and yellow crepe paper adorn the judge's bench. A four-foot cardboard turkey in full plumage is pasted to the witness stand.

The seven contesting relatives file into the courtroom. Each of the five men and two women wears an air of righteous indignation. Mr. O'Brien, the attorney Doug hired to represent our father, barely acknowledges us. I take this as a bad sign.

My father jiggles, twiddles his thumbs. "I made the wrong decisions and I've been on the wrong track all my life," he says to Gabriel.

Gabriel clears his throat. "I'd like your daughter's hand in marriage," he says.

"All rise," a court officer says, before my father can answer.

The judge comes in, a tall woman in her fifties, cool and impervious. The court comes to order. The accusation of the relatives is read: ". . . whereby the execution of the alleged Will of Hazel Johnson was procured by the fraud and undue influence of one Harry F. Sweeney."

The attorney for the relatives, Mr. Thrash, elaborates on the specifications of the contestants. "The testatrix, Hazel Johnson, lived in the house in question, and at the time of the execution of the Will in question, was in very poor physical and mental health," he drones. "The petitioner, Harry F. Sweeney, lived with the testatrix up to the time of her death. As her illness progressed, he embarked on a program of complete custody, domination, and coercion of the testatrix, designed—"

A bark erupts from my father, something between a sob and a cough. All heads turn toward him.

Mr. Thrash scarcely misses a beat. "—domination, and coercion of the testatrix," he says, louder this time, as if to punish my father for interrupting, "designed to obtain for himself her estate, thereby cutting off all her heirs and next of kin. He carried out his scheme right up to the time of her death by continued and close surveillance of the testatrix and by discouraging attempts by her heirs to see or communicate with her. He kept the testatrix constantly under heavy medication and sedation so as to keep her under the influence of his domination."

Fat in his three-piece suit, Mr. Thrash reminds me of my grandfather, my father's father, who buttoned his scratchy vest over his belly. I didn't have much to do with him, a tyrant who didn't like children.

My father is called to the stand for direct examination. Do the relatives believe the charges they've made against him? It hardly seems to matter—my father looks bad and can be made to look worse. He hobbles to the stand.

"Would you state your full name, sir?" Thrash says.

"Harry F. Sweeney," he says.

"How old are you, Mr. Sweeney?"

Five, I want to say. He's stuck there, a five-year-old in glasses, ridiculed by his father. He gives the shortest answers he can, so as not to incur further wrath.

"Sixty," he says.

"Married?"

"Divorced."

"Children?"

"Two."

"Boys or girls?"

My father sighs. "A boy and a girl."

A flash of anger illuminates the dark sadness inside me. He shouldn't have had children. How can I feel so sorry for him one minute, so angry with him the next? Gabriel reaches for my cold hand with his warm one, then slides over to me across my father's empty seat.

"During the time you knew Hazel Johnson, what were her physical troubles?" Thrash says.

"First she broke her hip," my father says. He speaks with difficulty, as if his memories are as painful as Hazel's afflictions were to her. "She fractured her back twice. She had pneumonia. They amputated both her legs because of her circulation problems."

I glance at Gabriel. His head is slightly bowed, like a priest's in a confessional.

"At that time you were living at her house?" Thrash says.

"Yes, because she asked me to," my father says.

"I was just asking if you lived there," Mr. Thrash sneers.

"Yes."

"Did you have your meals while you were there?"

"I did the grocery shopping, and we had a mutual—"

"You didn't pay any board?" Thrash says.

"No."

"You took care of her at night?"

"She was there alone, so I had to."

I didn't know where he was when he was taking care of Hazel. The abyss widens between my father's description of his life and Thrash's implications. Should I feel betrayed for my mother's sake?

Thrash paces back and forth. "Who was there when the will was signed?"

"A couple who were good friends of Mrs. Johnson," my father says, his voice quavering. "Mr. and Mrs. Cioletta."

"When did she call them as witnesses?"

"Her lawyer Mr. Gallagher called and asked her if he could come over that evening, it was told to me later, I didn't know at the time any of these things were going on, that if she could get two witnesses then he'd be over, and he could execute it at that time," he says. "So then she called them."

My father hovers between fear and indignation. He shrinks from Thrash, who keeps him off balance by his tone, his pacing, getting right in my father's face.

"That is what she told you?" Thrash says.

"I didn't say she told me! I think Mr. Gallagher told me, but I can't pinpoint exactly what happened. I know I didn't know anything about it in advance. That's what I'm trying to say." He sweats with confusion and fear. What if he collapses right on the stand?

"Where did you sleep?" Thrash presses.

"On a cot in the kitchen."

"This night that the Ciolettas and Mr. Gallagher were there, where was Mrs. Johnson?"

"In her wheelchair."

"Where was the will executed? Where were you?"

"I went out to the clothesline. There were a lot of clothes I'd washed in the morning, and I was taking them off the line and folding them."

"Had you discussed with Mrs. Johnson that Mr. Gallagher was coming?"

"No, because he had—"

"The answer is no," Mr. O'Brien, my father's lawyer, says. He raises his bushy white eyebrows.

"No," my father says.

"You want us to believe that you had no idea that Mr. Gallagher and the two witnesses were there for purposes of executing a will?" Thrash goes on.

"Yes, sir."

I know my father is telling the truth. Wistful he didn't take clothes from the line for us, I see him doing it for Hazel.

"Did you ever answer the phone when any of Mrs. Johnson's cousins called?" Thrash says.

"Her cousins never called."

"Did you ever tell anyone she was too sick to talk to him?" he says. He steps still closer to my father, crowds him, breathes in his face. "Did you ever do that?"

My father recoils. "No," he says.

"Did you give her medications up to her death?"

"Yes," he says. "I kept a chart day by day."

"You kept charts," Thrash says. "What would the charts consist of?"

"Times for the medications."

"Did the medications continue at the same prescribed frequencies from when she got home from the hospital up to the time she died?"

"I object to that kind of question," Mr. O'Brien says. "Are you referring to dosage?" He has a slight Irish brogue.

"You were there the night the will was signed, but knew

nothing of what was taking place, is that what you want us to believe?" Thrash says.

"I didn't want to get involved," my father says. "I didn't know what it was all about!"

"Just answer yes or no," Mr. O'Brien says. "Take it easy."

"Did you come back from folding the clothes while Mr. Gallagher was still there?" Thrash says.

"How do I remember all these little details?" my father says. He grows paler.

"Try to remember the best you can, and tell the man the best you can," Mr. O'Brien says. "Think real hard."

"What do you live on?" Thrash says, as if driving home his point.

"I eat frugally," he says. "I live frugally."

"You're homeless, are you not?" Thrash says.

My father withers. "Yes," he says.

My heart aches to realize he has lost track of what to be ashamed of, what not.

"Your wife—what is your former wife's name?" Thrash says.

"Louise." He inhales sharply.

"Your wife Louise divorced you on grounds of cruel and abusive treatment?" Thrash says.

"I object," Mr. O'Brien says.

My father puts his hand to his heart. He clutches the rail. I want to run to the stand to catch him.

"That will be all," Thrash says.

Mr. O'Brien runs his hand through his bushy white hair. His broad back toward us, he puts his papers back in his briefcase.

My father makes his way from the stand. He sways with grief, looks as if he doesn't know where he's going. If lost, relax, I want to tell him. He comes back to our bench, sits down.

"It's okay, Dad," I say. I put my hand on his arm.

Gabriel studies my father while we wait for the judge's decision. I search Gabriel's face for signs of concern and what kind.

"Who would've thought the one decent thing I did for somebody would turn out bad like everything else?" my father says.

I picture Hazel's house, bottles of pills on the window-sills, railings in the bathroom. "How did you find it in your-self to take such good care of her?" I say.

"You don't blame me for it?" he says.

"Of course not."

How does he bear her death? Is there time for grief in the chaos of his life? Maybe grief takes all his time. Like Chance and Reggie and Kathy, he seems in permanent mourning for one loss after another.

"I was responsible for her," he says, "and she was responsible for me."

I look at Gabriel; he looks at me. Whether Gabriel and I will share something like that depends somehow on whether I can accept this gift my father offers me. I struggle not to be jealous of a dead amputee who taught my father something we—my mother, my brother, and I—couldn't. But he learned it, didn't he? He'd want me to learn it too.

"I couldn't let you marry my daughter—" my father says, then stops when the judge begins to speak.

"I find that the will was properly executed and not the product of undue influence," the judge says. "I am entering an order admitting the will to probate."

"—but I see you're a pretty good guy," my father goes on, and shakes Gabriel's hand.

The three of us stand. We make our way past the defeated relatives.

After we take my father back to his convalescent home, Gabriel and I drive back to my mother's house. The November air is damp and gray.

"So what do you think?" I say.

"About what?"

"About my father."

I drive because it's too hard to tell Gabriel where to go. Boston grew without urban planning and Houston without zoning, but these deficiencies create two different kinds of problems. I feel my way toward my mother's house, around rotaries, under tiny bridges and over big ones, seemingly crossing the Charles River over and over again.

"What do *you* think of your father?" he says.

My father took Dougie and me to play along the Charles. We'd roll down the grassy bank, giggling and screaming. My father caught us before we fell into the river. We'd race up the bank to roll down again.

"It's not that my father didn't love us—"

I can drive and talk, but not drive and cry.

Gabriel looks over at me. He takes his clean white handkerchief out of his pocket and wipes my cheeks. Before Gabriel, I never knew a man who carried a handkerchief. Gabriel's are even monogrammed, while I'm a Kleenex kind of girl.

"It's okay," he says.

The Jamaicaway goes by in a blur of trees, joggers, bicyclists. Driving its curves is like dancing a waltz. I waltzed with Gabriel at the debutante cotillion. My father will never make me a debutante, but I do have a father.

"It wasn't all bad," I say. "Once my parents even loved each other. We'd all go to a drive-in movie, Dougie and I in our pajamas. Dougie fell asleep stretched across the back seat. I lay in the car's back window, and looked up at the moon and the stars."

Gabriel moves closer, puts his arm around me. Just like my parents did, long ago. Who would have thought that one of the most intimate things you could tell a man was something good about your parents instead of something bad?

14

Thanksgiving

Thanksgiving morning, I wake up to voices downstairs in the kitchen. Robert and Sidney always arrive early Thanksgiving Day so Robert can help my mother cook the turkey and Sidney can referee. I can't make out the words but I know they're having the same turkey argument they have every year. Robert thinks my mother overcooks the turkey and my mother tries to keep Robert from taking it out of the oven while it's still gobbling.

Gabriel slept in my brother's old room, and I slept in my old room, with its blue flowered wallpaper, white curtains and bedspread—a virgin's room. There's something both regressive and comforting about sleeping in a room that hasn't changed for years, when one has changed so much. After I dress, I go downstairs and am flabbergasted to see Gabriel at the kitchen sink, rinsing out the inside of the turkey.

"Good morning, Miss Princess-and-the-Pea," Robert says.

"'Morning, everybody," I say. "You're letting Gabriel help with the turkey when you never let me?"

"He's a doctor, dear," my mother says.

"I know this procedure," Gabriel says. "You had me put their turkey, stuffing, and gravy recipes in my safe deposit box, remember?"

"I don't want to lose them," I say.

In her Thanksgiving apron with the cornucopia on the front, my mother toasts squishy white Wonder Bread, then tears the slices into little pieces. Robert and Sidney could be the Brooks Brothers themselves in their khakis, pink oxford shirts with the tails hanging out, and Gucci loafers.

I can almost read the stock quotations on Robert's nose, covered with newsprint from this morning's *Times*. "How's the market?" I say.

"It was a madhouse yesterday afternoon," my mother says. "Everyone was buying their Butterballs."

"Falling," Robert says. He sautés the celery and onions for the stuffing.

His sleeves rolled up, Gabriel lightly pats the turkey cavity dry.

"Did Dalzenia let you help cook the turkey?" I ask him.

"My father and I *shot* the turkey," he says. "Dalzenia cleaned it, dressed it, and cooked it while Mother fussed endlessly with the place cards."

"How many possible seating arrangements were there for a family dinner?" I say.

"More than you might think," he says.

"Feel free to use the phone to wish your parents a happy Thanksgiving," my mother says to Gabriel. "Mothers like to hear from their children on holidays.

"They're celebrating it in London," he says. "Mother's forcing Thanksgiving on the British."

"That will serve the British right," my mother says. She

doesn't know how right she is. Peaches would have insisted on place cards at Plymouth Rock, not to mention the Boston Tea Party.

Helping to cook the turkey is a rite of passage I won't get to perform until my mother, Robert, or Sidney drops by the wayside and I'm called in as reinforcement. My fear is they'll all drop at once; that's why I keep recipes for the whole production in Gabriel's safe deposit box.

"Go set the table; you're making us nervous," Robert says.

My mother has only one set of china, for formal and everyday. The bridal registry consultant told me I'd have to register for both. I don't know whether to be sad for myself because I had to learn that, or sad for my mother because she'll never know. Robert and Sidney know; they have several sets, from estate sales and antique dealers. They have little dessert plates, fish plates and finger bowls, colored crystal with high lead content. They have silver Louis Quatorze grapefruit spoons, pearl-handled lunch and dinner forks from civilizations that have disappeared. Having adopted an alternative lifestyle, they have to be more correct than everyone else.

Robert and Sidney are my only model of a happily married couple. I sneak peeks at Gabriel as I shuttle back and forth between the dining room table and my mother's kitchen cabinets. I fold cloth napkins decoratively next to the plates. My mother has a gold tablecloth and napkins for Thanksgiving, red and green for Christmas, pink at Easter to go with the ham. When I was growing up, we had paper napkins. We didn't have napkins at all until I came home from camp for the first time. "They had *napkins*," I said to my mother. I don't know when she traded up to linen, but I'm relieved. What if I brought Gabriel home to paper napkins?

He was using paper towels when I first moved in, but I guess when you're born to damask you can take liberties like that. Maybe it's radical chic.

Sidney puts the giblets and neck in water, his eye on the clock.

"How long do the giblets have to cook?" I say.

"Forever," Robert says.

"Until Robert's Campari-and-gin," Sidney says. He doesn't let Robert have a drink until eleven.

Robert stuffs the turkey, pats it with oil, sprinkles it with paprika, but Gabriel gets to truss it.

"All because you went to medical school," I say.

Robert jockeys for position next to the turkey. "If you put it in now," he says to my mother, "Thanksgiving dinner will be brunch."

Sidney raises his warning finger at Robert. Before I knew Sidney was my aunt, I used to fantasize he'd marry my mother and save her from my father. Sidney and my mother used to stay up until all hours, dancing to Lester Lanin records around the empty glasses on the coffee table.

They put the turkey in the oven. Sidney stands between my mother and Robert and the stove. They mash potatoes, bake rolls, make cranberry relish and salad. They send me outside to gather autumn leaves for the centerpiece.

The cold November air braces me after the warmth of the kitchen. My mother's golden retriever follows me around the back yard, as if pleading with me to put in a good word for him. I hope my father gets Thanksgiving dinner at his convalescent home.

"Can Humphrey come in?" I say when I go back in.

"I completely forgot about him," my mother says.

Humphrey is so huge, so disruptive a presence, it's as if three more people crowd into the small kitchen. He jumps all over the others while I sidestep behind them. Gabriel lets Humphrey slobber all over him. I won't be able to bring myself to kiss Gabriel until he has had his next shower.

When everything's made but the gravy, Gabriel and I wander into the living room and sit down together on the sofa to wait for Doug, Pamela, and Chelsea. Humphrey sits at Gabriel's feet, waiting for his next kiss.

"There's no plan!" Gabriel says. "Y'all just hang out."

"We'll sit around and drink," I say. "*That's* the plan."

"They're self-medicating."

"That's one way of putting it."

"Holidays at my parents' start with church, followed by brunch at the country club, then visits to people we didn't see at the club," he says. "Then we assemble for a family portrait on the front lawn, followed by an afternoon party for two hundred of Mother's closest friends and their entire extended families, a non-optional game of croquet, a family dinner at home, songs around the piano, viewing of the last thirty years of family photos, and genteel conversation until bedtime. No one gets to retire until Mother wears out, which is never." He takes advantage of our moment alone to draw me to him.

I brace myself to kiss him through Humphrey's dog germs. "Don't doctors believe in the germ theory?"

"Millions of germs crawl all over everything all the time."

"That's reassuring."

"Humphrey ought to worry what he might get from us, rather than us what we might get from him," he says.

Humphrey cocks one ear.

"You'd be lucky to get Gabriel's germs," I tell him.

"Why does Sidney schedule Robert's drinks?" Gabriel says.

"Robert's going to go after someone," I say. "Sidney's trying to postpone that moment as long as possible."

"Go after whom?"

"Maybe Doug, maybe Sidney, probably you," I say. "Doug loves it, Sidney and my mother are used to it, I hate it, and it reduces Pamela to tears."

"Dominant males fighting for supremacy," Gabriel says.

"It isn't some anthropological tribal ritual," I say. "It's an Irish brawl."

"Did your father participate in this?" he says.

"He lost every time."

My father fell out of the loop, as far as my mother's family was concerned, back in my early childhood. They were a tight circle he was never able to penetrate. Will I be able to penetrate the Benedict family? When my mother's mother was alive, Robert and Sidney danced around Grandmother as if she were a maypole. She sat at her umbrella table on the back lawn, surrounded by zinnias and shasta daisies the same colors as the tall frosty aluminum tumblers of gin— orange, purple, pink. My pale grandfather waited on the others like a butler.

Robert comes into the living room and turns on the TV, but his favorite financial programs have been pre-empted by parades. Sidney hands him his Campari-and-gin.

"Now," Robert says, "let's talk about the wedding."

"Will you have a martini fountain?" Sidney asks me.

"But no dancing," my mother says. "I can't come if the bride's mother has to dance with the bride's father."

"Dad doesn't dance," I say.

My mother's afraid the wedding will force her into all sorts of southwestern tribal rituals. Robert and Sidney regard it simply as an odious public display of heterosexual Texan affection.

"Let's see your badge of servitude," Robert says to me.

They're admiring my engagement ring when Doug and Pamela arrive with Chelsea. The three of them blow vaporous breaths from the cold air outside. Pamela hands my mother a tray of hors d'oeuvres. Chelsea sits down hard next to Humphrey, leans up against him, her sofa.

"Did you know there's an overturned beetle in your driveway?" Pamela asks my mother.

"I ran over him with the Volvo," Doug says.

We start in on Pamela's mushroom caps and stuffed dates. Gabriel's eye wanders to a basketball game on TV, the Houston Rockets vs. the Boston Celtics.

"If you watch it, someone will interrupt you so you can't," I murmur to him.

"Shall I turn it off?" he says.

"They want it on so it seems someone's talking," I say.

"Any other rules I should know about?"

"You're supposed to drink attentively and listen to Robert, responding enough to give him ammunition to attack you later," I say. "But if I were you, I wouldn't."

The house fills with the smells of sage and onion, roasting turkey, squash pie.

"What do y'all do at the I.R.S.?" Gabriel asks Robert and Sidney.

"Throw little old ladies who can't pay their taxes in jail," Robert says.

"Help me make the gravy," Sidney says to Robert.

"How many people does it take to make gravy?" I say.

"One to put in the cornstarch and one to say 'no more,'" Sidney says.

I hear the creak of the oven door and know Robert is sneaking the turkey out of the oven. A few moments after he comes back I hear the creak again, my mother sneaking it back in.

"Can Chelsea make a decent martini yet?" Robert asks Doug. It's a family tradition for the youngest child to make the drinks after Sidney fires the starting gun at eleven.

"She still thinks the jigger is a rattle," Doug says.

"The jigger!" I say. "No one in this family has bothered with a jigger for years."

"That's enough out of you, Mother Mary Fudge-Cake," Robert says.

"I remember when you ate the olives out of our martinis," Sidney says to me.

"No one bothers with the olives anymore, either," I say. "They tasted of my childhood, like Proust's madeleines."

"Those soaked olives were a perfect waste of good gin," Robert says.

Pamela plays with Chelsea. They're in Laura Ashley mother-daughter outfits—white blouses with Peter Pan collars and dark flowered corduroy jumpers. It's too old for Chelsea and too young for Pamela. You can tell at which age a woman was traumatized by the way she dresses. Pamela recites to Chelsea the nursery rhyme about the little girl who had a little curl and was both very good and very horrid. If Pamela and I were one person, she'd be well-balanced. One of us is very good and it's not me.

Pamela asks Gabriel about Gabe, and his work in the E.R. Everyone likes Gabriel and is happy we're engaged, but Pamela aligns herself with him as a fellow interloper. I'm grateful for that.

No one else asks Gabriel about his family or his work, because they think it's impolite to show too much interest in someone. Instead, Robert baits Gabriel about the health care crisis. Robert is more Republican than the Republicans, while Gabriel is too busy taking care of his flood of indigent patients to be political.

"It doesn't mean what it used to, to be a Republican or a Democrat," I say.

"None of us have been Democrats for years," Robert says.

"Not since we moved out of the lower middle class," my mother says.

"*I* was never lower middle class," Robert says.

"We were poor in our childhood," my mother says to him. "My children and I rose from that to lower middle class."

"I rose directly from poor to upper class," Robert says.

I choke on a stuffed mushroom cap with the vision of Robert ascending on a cloud like Christ after the Resurrection.

His Campari-and-gins have gone from the deeper shades of rose to the delicate, wispy ones, as if the pink has been evaporating from his drinks. When it's just gin cracking the packed ice in his glass, he waves the vermouth over it and they all switch to martinis.

"They won't trust you if you don't drink," I whisper to Gabriel.

"Is there a Lone Star longneck?" he says. He wants to be both honest and agreeably participatory.

"They've never heard of Lone Star." I hand him some ice water, which looks like a martini in the right stemmed glass.

"Whispering sweet nothings, my little turtle doves?" Robert says to us. He sniffs. Humphrey lifts his head and sniffs also. Robert jumps up, stalks into the kitchen and tears the turkey out of the oven.

"It's still cold," my mother calls to him.

"If you can smell it, it's done," Robert says.

Sidney hugs my mother in a conciliatory way; she shrugs and smiles. We take our places around the dining room table, my mother at the end closer to the kitchen and Robert at the other end. Doug and Pamela used to want to sit next to each other but now Chelsea's ensconced between them.

"How do people stay married?" Gabriel asks Doug.

"They take on big debts," Doug says.

"I took on big debts but they didn't help me," he says.

"You could afford to get out," Doug says.

"I'm your karmic debt," I say to Gabriel. I sit at the right hand of Robert, my surrogate father since my father fell so irremediably from grace.

"Sit down, Sidney," Robert says to him as he carves the turkey.

Sidney stands at the window and watches the neighbor's children put nail-studded boards under people's cars. "Mercy," he says.

"They're not evil children—the whole family is just stupid," my mother says. She passes around the potatoes and cranberries. "The mother lets them run wild. I told her I saw her two-year-old playing in the Stop & Shop parking lot and she just said 'He's all right.' I think she's hoping they'll get killed."

"What are you going to do when they blow out your tires, darling?" Sidney asks her.

"I'm excellent with stupid people," my mother says. "I'm going to pay the older kids to help me trim the hedge and get them on my side."

Gabriel bows his head for grace until he realizes no one's going to say it.

"Drumstick or breast?" Robert asks my mother.

"Breast, please," my mother says. "The mother is a nymphomaniac. One of her boyfriends got jealous and tried to burn down the house."

"That's how whole families become homeless," I say.

"The homeless have a hypertrophic sense of entitlement," Robert says, briskly clipping his words. He affects a British accent when he starts to feel sloshed.

"They don't feel entitled to anything," I say. "That's the trouble." I fling myself into the argument to keep Gabriel out of it.

"They should work their way up, like we did," Doug says.

"They lack outer and inner resources," I say. I think of Chance, Reggie and Kathy, Sandra. "They don't have our blessings."

"They won't get mine," Robert says. He holds my plate midair as if he's not going to give it back.

"What's the problem as you see it?" I say.

"Overpopulation, especially among minorities!" Sidney says. "People who can't afford children shouldn't have them."

"We have to do what we can for the people who are already here," I say.

"Why do something for a few when thousands more are born every day?" Robert says. He swallows a mouthful of turkey.

"What are *you* doing to alleviate the problem?" Doug asks me.

"I'm not overpopulating and I'm not criticizing the people who are trying to help," I say. If I told them about my homeless proposal they'd send me to my room.

"Don't be a fruitcake," Robert says.

"I'm not overpopulating either," Doug says. "I'm glad we had a girl so we can end the family line."

"Chelsea's being female doesn't end the family line," I say.

Sexism, racism, and class struggles all in the same dinner.

Impervious, Pamela feeds Chelsea. Gabriel's head whips back and forth as if he's at an exciting basketball game. I hear the game in the background; the TV is still on. How will I explain to Gabriel that instead of talking about what's really bothering them, my family expresses feelings in political metaphor? They draw battle lines between the Republicans and the Democrats instead of the straight and the gay, the happy and the unhappy, the living and the dead.

"Let's not end Thanksgiving dinner in a brawl," my mother says, after we've squabbled our way through several helpings. "Help me clear the table, Mother Teresa."

"Robert doesn't want to understand your argument, he only wants to win," Pamela whispers as I pick up her plate.

"Don't be so sensitive, dear," my mother says to me out in the kitchen. "You know how Robert likes to stir things up."

Doug and Pamela excuse themselves to have dessert with friends. They leave Chelsea with us. She sits in her high chair and throws Cheerios at Robert. My mother starts the coffee, heats the pie in the oven. I take the ice cream out of the freezer so we'll be able to get a spoon into it.

Humphrey bounds into the kitchen from where he has been hiding under the dining room table.

"How did Humphrey smell the i-c-e c-r-e-a-m when I haven't even taken off the lid?" I ask my mother.

"He can spell it, too," my mother says.

"Can you talk some sense into her about the homeless?" Robert says to Gabriel while we eat our pie and ice cream.

"I plead the Fifth," Gabriel says, and raises both his hands. He likes to discuss, but not to argue.

"He doesn't have to fight with us," I say.

"Indeed?" Robert says.

"Listen to us sometime when we're all shouting," I say.

"Nobody makes any sense or listens to anyone else. Before you know it, we're all drunk and the drunker we get the less sense we make."

"I'm *never* drunk," Robert says.

"But that's how we have fun," my mother says. "It's how we're a family."

"It's not everyone's idea of fun or family," I say. I wince to remember my faux pas at the Benedicts' brunch.

"Mother Mary Fudge-Cake again," Robert says.

"Can't you imagine another point of view?" I say.

"Not when I'm right, and you're wrong, wrong, wrong," he says. He stirs his drink with the ice cube tongs.

My mother feeds Chelsea tiny pieces of squash pie while her own grows cold. Chelsea screeches between each mouthful. She's at that pre-verbal stage with many opinions about the world but no words to speak them.

"Why can't she just ask for whatever she wants?" Robert says. "Couldn't she just point or something?"

She screeches again—a long, high squawk, like a furious turkey.

Robert drops the tongs, puts both hands on the table, and screeches back. Chelsea stops mid-screech and stares at him. She screeches again. Robert shrieks back. "You help too," he says to me.

"Yiiieeeeeee!" I say, in spite of myself.

"Screeeeeech!" Chelsea says.

"Aaaaiiiiiiiieeeeeeee!" Robert says.

"You'll scare her," my mother says.

But Chelsea's thrilled. She pounds her highchair tray with her chubby little palms.

Robert bangs on the dinner table; the plates and silverware bounce up and down.

Gabriel looks at us in amazement.

"Is this primal screaming?" I say. It feels too good to stop.

"Give me four hours with this baby," Robert says. "I'd have her straightened out in no time. This is a far cry from all that ga-ga and goo-goo Doug and Pamela pull on this kid."

"Mercy," Sidney says.

"If you tell Doug and Pamela," Robert says to him, "we've had it."

"Stop!" my mother says. "The neighbors will think we're killing each other and they'll call the police."

By the time Doug and Pamela get back, Chelsea's little mouth is wrapped around her bottle. My mother holds her in her lap, and we all sit there quietly as if nothing has happened. We have a nightcap—milk-and-whiskeys for everyone but no whiskey for Chelsea.

I'm penitent about the screaming match Robert and I had with Chelsea. She seems to me a small, innocent part of myself that I can't afford to be, and that Robert has no tolerance for in himself.

"Would you shriek back at Gabe like that?" Gabriel says to me.

"Gabe wouldn't shriek," I say. Isn't that the difference between our families, right there?

15

Sleeping Under the Drive-Through Bank

"I want a white female substance abuser," Vanessa says, reading me the riot act about whom she wants in our homeless study. "I want an African-American veteran with Gulf War syndrome, a male prostitute with AIDS, a runaway Asian teenager, an umemployed single mother, a battered mentally ill older adult, and an undocumented Latino family."

"Those aren't the real categories," I say. "My African-American is an unemployed substance abuser with mental-health problems. My runaway is a white male pimp, and my prostitute is a female HIV-positive incest survivor. My single mother is a battered day-laborer, and my undocumented family is twelve boat people who won't tell me whether they're related or not."

She gazes out her window to the street. "That proves how intractable the homeless problem really is."

"Try sorting out library services for them."

"Now don't pull attitude, girlfriend," she says, and turns back to me. "The public would rather assuage its conscience with the library's Service-to-the-Unserved than with the more costly basic services the homeless really need."

"Everyone's annoyed with the people they want to help," I say. How do I explain to Vanessa how ashamed I am of the way my frustration reveals my own prejudices to me?

She pulverizes me with the stare that earned the trustees' admiration. "Do you believe the homeless can be socialized to library use?"

"They might if we have homeless story hours, do attractive homeless bulletin boards, and expand the homeless Dewey decimal classification," I say, as if I read it in *Library Journal*.

"What about the ones we'll always have to go to because they won't come to us?"

"When people come to the library, they have to follow our rules," I say. "When we go to our three hundred homebound people, we have to follow three hundred sets of rules. But when we go to the homeless, all the rules are up for grabs."

This is hard for Vanessa and me to comprehend. We've loved rules all our lives. We're like people who know so many computer languages they can access any database. When we've maxed out on one set of rules, we eagerly switch to another.

"Supplement the study with polka-dotted Martians if you want to," she says, "but cover the politically correct populations."

Chance calls to say he found a whole family sleeping under the overhang of a drive-through bank. Even at the bank, Houstonians don't get out of their cars. Chance is taking the family to a homeless shelter, and wants me to meet him there.

Melissa Swanson, the shelter's social worker, has salt-and-pepper hair and lines around her mouth from her world-weary smile. When I get there, she's handing out pillow cases, each with a set of sheets, a towel, a washcloth, and a bar of soap inside, to the family of five.

"Are you hungry?" she asks them. She takes them to the shelter's dining hall for sandwiches.

"How does a family like this become homeless?" I ask Chance as we watch them trudge down the hall—a discouraged father, an exhausted mother, three disheveled children. The oldest child, a girl of about nine, reminds me of myself at her age—skinny, worried, knobby-kneed in what must be her only shorts and a sleeveless blouse. She has one of her brothers in tow, a wide-eyed little boy about Gabe's age. The mother carries the baby, a sad-looking one-year-old with scrapes and bruises on his face and arms.

"Loss of their income, no jobs," Chance says. "You lose this here, so your pride is dropped. So you go to a lower place, and you still can't keep that up, because you got to be took care of, the kids got to be took care of too. Also the clothes, the transportation. The rent lady's not going to take no pity on you because you got kids. They want they money, so you get out, then where do you go from there? Your kids hanging on to you, your belongings in your hand. Then your kids asking why they not over there no more, what's happening. They can't understand and that's breaking you down, and they ain't nobody to help you. That's why a lot of people become homeless, they just ain't got no help. The right people is out there, but what I'm saying is, it's not enough to help over here, here, and there."

"It must make a person pretty desperate," I say.

"That's why a lot of crime going on," he says. "They don't be having it in their heart to do nothing wrong. Understan' me, but you think about it, if you went three days sleeping here and there, and you not a person that want to go stealing nothing, but then also you haven't ate in three days, and things going rough for you. You're not really no robber, when your stomach get talking to you, your mind is out of control. You know what I'm talking about? So if they take a little something here, a little something there, not like a drug addict, it's not that, it be because they *hungry*. You know if a person have a lot of money, and they lost so much, they turn to alcohol, they try to drink they problems away, y'understand what I'm saying? It's like fooling with smoke and crack. It just be like, don't nobody care, what can we do? A lot of people with different types of problems, they try different things to take it off they minds."

I search Chance's face, shiny with sweat, puffy with sleeplessness. "Are you still taking your medication and looking for a job?"

"You still getting hitched?"

"Yes," I say. "Are you going to make it to my wedding?"

"If it wasn't for folks like these here at the shelter," he says, avoiding my eyes, "this whole city be flipped upside down. It's the good folks that care about the homeless. The people of God, the people that got God in their hearts. Not them riding past you, saying 'Lock your doors, them people might rob you.'"

I give Chance what I've saved for his hot dog fund. He protests that he would have brought the family here anyway, but I appreciate his insightful analysis. The family was too shell-shocked for me to talk to myself. He slips away.

Melissa comes back to give me a quick tour, all she has time for with a waiting room full of desperate men, women, and children. The clean, spartan rooms and posted lists of rules and regulations remind me of my college dormitory, but it's not like going away to college. I keep an eye out for a quiet alcove that could serve as a library outpost, wonder what library materials would help.

A woman stops us in the hall to ask for some denture adhesive. When Melissa gives it to her it's obvious how much it means to her. What would it be like to have nothing and be grateful for the barest essentials?

"Combs, brushes, toothpaste, we have all that," Melissa tells me. "Diapers, shampoo. We make referrals to other agencies for job training, employment, health care, whatever we can't provide ourselves. We try to be a temporary refuge for people trying to get on their feet, without fostering long-term dependency."

"Does it work?"

"We have some good success stories," she says. "We have people right out of jail to whom we say let's forget about the past and go from here, and they get a job and a place to live and move out. Other people break all the rules, from smoking in their rooms to not taking care of their children. The more you correct them the more they deteriorate, and on the way out they're calling us names and throwing things at us."

"Do the children go to school?" I say.

"A neighborhood school takes our kids at all times of the year," she says. "We give the kids school supplies, but they're upset, their families falling apart. A lot of them don't even know their fathers; the siblings all have different fathers. There's a certain amount of security in knowing you have a mother and a father and they live in the same place and you're all going to love each other."

Is there a family like that left in America? "Can you see homeless people using the library as a resource?" I say.

"Some of them," she says, "those you can help to help themselves. Others are too hungry, too beaten down."

This whole project is wearing me down. I see my homeless study going down the tubes, my job with it.

Melissa must read the look on my face. "Homeless people face problems different from yours and mine," she says. "But like us, they either have or don't have the emotional resources to cope with them."

"What do you mean?"

"Their daily lives are so complex and harassed, it's hard to do the simplest things like go to the grocery store. Going to the public health clinic is an eight-hour process. Some are not only working through their problems but helping other people with worse ones."

She leads me out through the dining room, where the family from under the drive-through bank sits with hundreds of other people. The man and three children eat hungrily, dazed. The woman cries, her head down on the table.

Melissa stops to put her hand on the woman's shoulder. "You're going to hang on," Melissa tells her. "You *can't* give up now. We'll figure it out; we always do."

The woman looks up at her, dubious.

"We have to talk," Gigi says when she calls me at the library. "I'm so depressed." She finally met Malcolm, the man she fell in love with on the information superhighway, in person.

"Meet me at Chuy's during happy hour," I say. With its shrine to Elvis Presley and its Tex-Mex food, Chuy's is the sort of place you feel happy in even if you're miserable.

Gigi and I order frozen margaritas at the bar, once we've elbowed our way through the roaring crowd. "With salt!" I shout to the bartender.

"We can't talk in here," Gigi says to me.

I follow her out the door, past the sign that says it's against the law to take alcohol outside. I point this out as we sit down on a bench.

"What are they going to do, arrest us?" she says.

"We might get a ticket or something."

"We can't get a ticket for drinking a margarita," she says. Nevertheless, she hides our drinks behind her purse. "We don't want the other people out here to be unhappy we have a drink and they don't."

The bouncer comes up and says we have to take our drinks inside.

Gigi flashes him her best smile. "Okay," she says. She doesn't move.

I'm nervous but I want to hear what's bothering her.

"Malcolm and I had a fabulous date—dinner, dancing, the works," she says. "Then he dropped the bad news."

"He's married?" I say. "Gay?"

"Worse than that."

"Married *and* gay?"

"*The* problem," she says. "The big one."

"AIDS."

"No!" she says. "The *mechanical* problem."

"Oh."

"I mean, I'm supposed to get down on my hands and knees and help this guy with this?" she says. "Give me a break."

"On your knees?"

"Whatever."

"Maybe there are other things you could try," I say.

"Not sex videos," she says. "They turned me off and he still didn't get turned on."

"There's more here than meets the eye."

"I told him he had to get a pump," she says, "but then he'd be hard all the time."

"That might not be so bad," I say.

"I have to figure out whether I like him enough to go through all this.

"Do you like talking to him?"

"On the computer."

"That's going to cause problems with your sex life."

"What sex life?" she says. "I'm jealous of that woman who had a dolphin in a marine park come on to her."

"You don't want to do it with a dolphin."

"The dolphin wouldn't let the woman out of the pool."

I stand up when the bouncer comes back again to tell us to move inside. "Life is too short to get arrested over a margarita," I say.

"We're all sexually challenged one way or another," she says. She follows me in. "But Gabriel obviously adores you."

I'm quiet for a moment, thinking about this.

"Are you getting ready to cry?" Gigi says.

"Of course not. I haven't cried much since I moved in with Gabriel."

The truth is, the only time I cry now is with excess of pleasure. Gabriel and I ought to pace ourselves when we make love, but we can't stand to wait that long. Our bedroom is fragrant with pleasure and love, rich scents like violets, cardamom. I get all hot and bothered just thinking of him—the way his body feels so close to mine, how hungry he makes me to look and touch, the way he pulls me closer still. He gives me so much of himself, I can't get enough of him.

Tonight I'll look into his eyes as long as he'll let me. I'll savor his aphrodisiac scent, brush my lips across his blond, furry skin. He'll kiss me all over, urged on by my soft, high cries.

"It's just that I'm surprised, quite honestly," Gigi says. "Not that Gabriel hasn't done something to make you cry, but that you haven't done something to make him give you something to cry about."

"Gabriel comforts me if I get upset," I say. "It startled me at first—I've never thought of it as something a man could do for a woman. Web's idea of comfort was to take me to an orgy."

"Web tried to distract you with a new problem so you couldn't solve the one at hand," she says. "Malcolm cares about me so much that when I'm with him I don't have fun but I feel good about myself."

"You'll have to find some way besides sex to have fun. What does Malcolm do to enjoy himself?"

"Seduces women by computer," she says. "What's Gabriel's idea of fun?"

"Besides catalogs, he reads Jung and gets his archetypes all stirred up."

"Men make a big mistake trying to access their feelings," she says. "They need us to tell them how they feel."

"What do you think men are good for?"

"They're cute," she says after thinking about it. "In everything else they need a lot of guidance and supervision."

"They mean well," I say. "Although sometimes Gabriel thinks I want to make sex too complicated."

"You don't want him to think that," she says. "If it's too complicated with you, he'll go have simple sex with somebody else."

"Maybe Prince Charles didn't make love long enough with Princess Di," I say.

"How long do you want it to take?"

"A day would be nice," I say. "From foreplay to afterglow."

"A day? How much foreplay?"

"Half a day."

"A whole half-day?" she says. "What do you expect him to do for half of a whole day?"

"An hour of kissing, an hour of hugging, and two hours of—whatever."

Gigi chokes on her frozen margarita. "The poor guy will get lockjaw," she says. "Or carpal tunnel syndrome, depending."

"I want all the stages I missed between hand-holding with the altar boys and kinky sex with Web."

"You have to make allowances for Gabriel. His job description includes reattaching penises cut off by angry wives."

Chuy's is full of couples totally focused on mating. I look around and wonder whether anyone else ever had this problem.

"Are you going to hire a decoy?" Gigi says.

"For ducks?"

"A gorgeous blonde to see whether Gabriel is faithful to you," she says. "It's a whole new business."

"I wouldn't have said I'd marry him if I weren't well on the way to trusting him."

Gigi finishes her margarita. "I'd better go," she says. "I have such early-morning meetings I get dressed while driving to work."

"In your BMW?"

"I've got to replace it with a truck. The guys driving by in pickups can see me putting on my pantyhose."

"In traffic?"

"Anyone can get dressed going only thirty," she says. "I have to do something with my rush hour."

"When you get killed, all you'll be known for was being busy."

"Nothing worse than using my black eyeliner as lipliner has happened."

"You should at least put on your pantyhose at home," I say.

"Mine are always drying on my car air-conditioner vents," she says. "It takes pantyhose three days to dry in Houston."

16

Within the Ribbon

"Gabriel, you have made me so happy," Peaches says when we call to tell her and King we're engaged.

"That's why I did it, Mother." Gabriel put off telling her for two months because he couldn't deal with a party.

"We'll have your engagement party here this Sunday afternoon," she says. "A tea, at four o clock." She hangs up.

"I'll call her back and tell her we can't make it," Gabriel says. He holds the receiver like a revolver in his hand.

"But it's my debut to Fort Worth society," I say. "What shall I wear?"

"You go," he says. "I'll stay home and work in the E.R."

"I'll help you have fun."

"Your family's glad we're engaged, but nobody's making a big deal out of it."

"Mine is not a family in which marriage is something to celebrate."

"Mother sees marriage strictly in terms of parties."

"My family has brawls; your family has parties."

"I'd trade with you any day."

"Instead of getting married, why don't we just switch families?"

Gabriel's still in a foul mood when we drive to Fort Worth early Saturday morning.

"If Southerners call Northerners 'Yankees,'" I ask him, "what should Northerners call Southerners?"

"'Sir' and 'Ma'am,'" he says.

"If the Yankees came over on the *Mayflower*," I say. "What did the Southerners come over on?"

"The *Niña,* the *Pinta,* and the *Santa Maria.*"

"They did not."

"The *Mayflower* didn't let the Northerners off at Plymouth Rock, then go 'round to let the Southerners off at the mouth of the Mississippi River," he says.

"So Southerners are actually descended from Yankees."

"We don't like people to make fun of our heritage."

I don't know how to deal with Gabriel when he's like this. Is it a guy thing, a doctor thing, a divorce thing, or a Texas thing?

"Is Texas part of the South or the West?" I say.

"Texas is Texas," he says. He glares at me. "Ever since the Revolution."

"Against Great Britain?" I say. I'm at a distinct disadvantage. In Massachusetts we have history up the wazoo so we take it for granted, where Texans make the most of what history they have.

"Against Mexico," he says. "Ever hear of the Alamo? Ever hear of Davy Crockett?"

"My brother had a Davy Crockett cap," I say.

"Ever hear of Jim Bowie?"

"He had a Bowie knife too," I say. "What happened in y'all's war?"

"One hundred and eighty-two Texans died defending the Alamo against five thousand Mexican soldiers, raising the battle cry that created the Republic of Texas," he says. "That never happened in your war."

I picture Gabriel in a buckskin doctor's coat and coonskin cap, wielding a musket. "If the thirteen colonies hadn't won their independence from Great Britain," I say, "Texas would be—"

"Independent and very rich," he says.

"There wouldn't have been a United States for Texas to become one of," I say.

"We invited y'all to merge with *us,*" he says.

In Fort Worth, Peaches drives me to a day spa, where she's treating me to a Day of Beauty. "You have *got* to make Gabriel cut his *beard,*" she says in the car. "He looks like someone people won't let *in* places. Felicity made a mess of him after I dressed him and taught him his manners."

She drives recklessly, distractedly. Her huge diamond ring blinks like a traffic light as she flicks her cigarette ashes out the window. The seatbelt warning squawks for blocks; the seatbelts of her Mercedes disappeared into the leather seats long ago.

We pass swankienda after swankienda bordered by dormant azalea bushes tended by gardeners. Texans spend fifty weeks a year fertilizing, watering, and pruning the azaleas for two weeks of blooming.

"Let me tell you about azaleas," Peaches says. "They are not a native Texas plant."

"Do you have a gardener?" I say.

"That would be stretchin' it," she says. "I have a man."

She pulls up to the spa but has something portentous to

tell me. "I have written to your mother," she says. "But I have not received a reply."

I picture my mother staring at Peaches's monogrammed note. Not only won't she understand what Peaches is saying with Southern indirectness, she won't know a reply is expected. I had to write my mother's notes to my teacher when I was absent from school. Peaches won't understand Yankee reserve, never mind my mother's shyness. I'd write Peaches a note on my mother's stationery, but my mother doesn't have any.

I sit there like a child who won't answer because she doesn't know what to say. Finally Peaches releases the Mercedes' child-proof door lock to let me out, then goes home to supervise preparations for tomorrow's engagement party.

The spa attendant ushers me into a white dressing room with gold satin hangers for my clothes. "This is for your lingerie," she says, and hands me a gold satin bag. She leaves me alone to change into a long white terry cloth robe. I'm naked under it, but that's the drill. When I step outside the dressing room, she asks whether I'd care for a glass of lemon water.

"Lemon water?" I say. I'm burning out on distinctions that could be historical, ethnic, class, or regional.

She escorts me to my first appointment. "Your mama-in-law-to-be has scheduled a full Day of Beauty for you." She affixes something like a dance card to my wrist. "You'll be a noodle when you walk out of here late this afternoon."

When someone strong-willed has the money to enforce it, the power shifts heavily in her direction. My first appointment is for the steam cabinet. I sit in the steam, wonder what Peaches will want in return. Will I be able to give it?

In the shower, I try to wash off my doubts. Everything is

provided to do so, from loofah sponge to exotic soaps. I lie down for my massage. I'm the one with the trust issues, but how can I trust anyone with the rest of my life? Gabriel must be worried too.

After my massage, I get a pedicure from Rhonda.

"When was the last time you had a pedicure?" Rhonda says and frowns at my feet.

"I can't remember." Have I ever had a pedicure?

"You're lucky you don't have ticklish feet. This is torture for some people."

"I can imagine."

I'm handed over for a hair consultation, shampoo, and cut. I'm served lunch under the hairdryer. I didn't know there still were hairdryers. Lunch is tiny sandwiches on white bread with the crusts cut off, little pickles, fresh pineapple slices and frozen grapes, biscotti, cappuccino.

After lunch I get my manicure and facial. I'm as helpless as a hospital patient, walking with cotton between my polished toes, trying to keep my robe closed with wet fingernails, stiff-faced and speechless with a facial mask.

Even stripped of his assets by Felicity, Gabriel will never be poor as I was, could be again. People like him never run out of money; dividends sprout not just from his investments but parents, education, doctor's salary and prestige. What if he grows as stubborn about sex as he is about the Texas Revolution? My ancestors weren't even here during the American Revolution. They came over on the coffin ships during the Irish potato famine. Who won the sexual revolution?

Finally, Marie gives me my makeup lesson and Alyssa does my comb-out. "If your life falls apart," Alyssa says, "it's because your hair is wrong."

It's a big-hair day. All I can see when I look in the mirror is how indebted I look.

"Do you like what they did to me?" I ask Gabriel back at Peaches and King's.

"I'll get used to it," he says.

"You won't have to, I could never do this myself. Tonight I'll sleep sitting up so I won't mess it up before the party."

"Father wants to see us in his den."

"What for?"

"He has a wedding gift for us," he says, "but first he wants to know whether we'll appreciate it."

We sit down in the panelled room, surrounded by King's hunting trophies. Air conditioning refrigerates the den so that we can have a roaring fire in the fireplace. Sixteen deer heads stare down from the walls. Perfectly preserved, bears lunge at us from the four corners. The taxidermist must have retired on this room alone. How did he remove all signs of gore?

King strides to a tall gun cabinet along one wall. He unlocks it and lifts down a hunting rifle. He's going to shoot me because I'm a Yankee.

"How's this strike your fancy?" he says.

"Is it loaded?" I say. If he gives it to us, we'll need a gun cabinet instead of a china cabinet.

"This was Gabriel's first rifle."

My stomach flips like a rabbit shot into the air, as it did when Gabriel introduced me to Felicity. Gabriel comes to me all of a piece with a history of hunting and marriage.

"These were Gabriel's too," King goes on, and points to five in all. "Boy's got to learn to hunt. In the fall we'd go dove-huntin', in open fields of maize. Gabriel learned to

shoot with a twenty-gauge single-shell shotgun. 'There's
one!' I'd say, and he'd fire, and I'd fire a few rounds with my
twenty-five-gauge. 'You got him!' I'd tell him, when one fell
to the ground." King grins; Gabriel smiles in spite of himself.

"Where'd you shoot the deer?" I ask. What I want to
know is why.

"On the ranch," he says. "First thing we'd do when we
get there, was sight the high-powered rifles. Then we'd drive
around in the Jeep, looking for deer."

Gabriel's face is a mix of nostalgia and horror. He must
have liked wearing rugged hunting clothes, stomping around
in the cool fall air, the camaraderie of the men. But I can't
picture him shooting animals. Instead I see him, resolute and
heartbroken, bending over broken creatures in the emergency room, sopping blood, pushing organs back in, stitch-
ing wounds.

"Colleen isn't fond of rifles," Gabriel says.

"This gun collection has been in the family for years,"
King says.

Gabriel shrugs. What can you do with old guns? Gabriel
won't sell or give them away; he can't donate them to the
Salvation Army. He'll suggest they be taken apart, the metal
and wood recycled, but King isn't one for recycling. Maybe
the best place for them is locked in King's gun cabinet. It's as
if King is trying to figure out who his son is now, after one
marriage and divorce, engaged to a Yankee. King and
Peaches are the kind of people who stay married no matter
what.

The largest wall trophy, a moose with enormous antlers,
gazes down at us. The moose's eyes remind me of my
father's.

"Did you shoot deer?" I ask Gabriel as we go up to dress
for dinner.

"Yes."

"How?"

"Right behind the shoulder," he says. "Bucks, not does. We'd count the points to make sure the buck was old enough."

"Old enough to die?" I say.

"Old enough he'd reproduced, lived a full life," he says. "The more points, the bigger the trophy."

We go to dinner at the country club.

"I feel loved and cared for at the club," Peaches says. "They care whether I'm happy or not."

"We all care whether you're happy, Peaches," King says.

"One of these dinners could feed a homeless family for a week," I say to Gabriel behind my menu.

Peaches is determined to plan the wedding over dinner. "Who on your side do you want within the ribbon?" she says.

"Within what ribbon?" I say.

I know my family and I are supposed to plan the wedding, but I don't know what I'm doing. My mother lacks the confidence to claim this motherly privilege, while Peaches has so much she seizes someone else's. King stands back and lets her do it. Gabriel acts as if he'll be doing a lot to show up at the altar. The more this becomes his mother's wedding, the less he'll want to do that.

"Beribboned pews for family, of course," Peaches says. "It says 'Within the Ribbon' on a card in their invitations." She adds the names of my relatives to her list of Gabriel's.

"Dalzenia too, of course," I say.

"To serve?" she says.

"Within the ribbon," I say.

"We'll have the wedding at the biggest church with the

prettiest center aisle," she says. "We'll have the rehearsal dinner at the Petroleum Club, the wedding breakfast at the Fort Worth Club, and the reception here at our country club. Y'all will spend your wedding night at the Stockyards Hotel, and—"

"Hold it, Mother," Gabriel says. "We're having the wedding in Houston, where our friends are."

"Our friends and the people you grew up with are here in Fort Worth," she says. "We'll fly up your Houston friends."

It'll be like being flown to Hollywood for a première. Gigi and our friends will love it.

"Maybe not," Gabriel says.

"Let's talk cake," she says. She's a Texan Marie Antoinette. She insists on a twelve-layer white cake with filigreed butter icing, cascading with marzipan magnolia blossoms and topped with silver bells encircling an ornamental bride and groom on horseback.

"Twelve layers?" I say.

"More would be Houstontatious," she says. "Will our groom's cake be traditional chocolate?"

"What's a groom's cake?" I say.

"Red velvet cake in the shape of an armadillo, with gray icing," King says.

"We are *not* havin' an armadilla groom's cake," Peaches says.

"I had an armadillo groom's cake," King says. "My father had an armadillo groom's cake, my father's father had an armadillo groom's cake, and Gabriel is going to have an armadillo groom's cake."

For a split second, Peaches is speechless.

"Did you have an armadillo groom's cake when you married Felicity?" I ask Gabriel.

"No," King says. "That was the trouble."

"Gabe will have an armadillo groom's cake," Gabriel says to me.

"Good," I say.

"Don't worry," Peaches says to me as we freshen our lipstick in the powder room. "If Gabriel insists on having the wedding and all the parties in Houston, my sister Pi Beta Phi's there will take care of everything."

We talk to each other in the mirror.

"Houston is having a bridal expo soon," I say. "I'll shop there for wedding services."

"People like us don't go to bridal expositions," she says. "We already know the best caterer, the best florist, the best everything."

After dessert, we're served flutes of pink champagne. Peaches and I drink our own, then King's and Gabriel's.

"I'm the designated drinker," I say to Gabriel.

He frowns at my being too festive.

"Being out with you is like being out with a supervisor," I tell him that night in the hallway between our two rooms. "What's wrong with a little *joie de vivre?*"

"I'd be happy if I just got the *vivre,*" he says. "I wish you hadn't worn those see-through pants."

"They're not see-through, they're diaphanous."

"You look like a strumpet," he says. Leave it to Gabriel to find the most genteel word to insult me.

Still, it hurts. "You're flaunting sex," my mother said when I wore miniskirts and my first bikini. "You can't expect me to approve of what you're doing." She stopped speaking to me for years.

"You're in a fashion vacuum," I say to Gabriel. "This is what everyone's wearing in the women's magazines. I look like a doctor's wife."

"You look like you're looking for another doctor," he says.

We separate to go to bed. Silence blares from his room all night. I feel as if I'm trying to steal him away from something, but I'm not going to get away with it.

Sunday morning, I throw myself into helping with the engagement party preparations. While Gabriel and King are at church, Peaches goes over the list of who'll pour tea at the party. The scheduling sounds complicated, with a change of shift every seven minutes for three hours.

"How does that work?" I say.

"Only the groom's mother's dearest friends are invited to pour tea," she says. "That's how people know who's a close friend of the family, by who gets to pour."

Dalzenia has been polishing Peaches's tea service for days, and now she sets it up on a damask-covered table in the garden. Festoons of oleander blossoms, from deep red to pure white, decorate the thirty little tables around the pool.

The caterers arrive, then the bartenders, then the valet parkers. Someone installs a massive ice sculpture of Gabriel and me outside on the tea table.

Still smarting from Gabriel's disapproval of my diaphanous pants, I'm dressed so conservatively I feel positively Baptist.

"Am I the way you like me?" I ask Gabriel.

"You're the way I can get you today."

Peaches lines us up in a receiving line in the foyer. "Gabriel stands next to me," she says, and sends King to the other end.

"She's just per-fect," people I never saw before say to Peaches.

"When do we get to go to the party?" I ask Gabriel.

"We don't. It comes to us."

"Why do the servers rush over when I smile at them?"

"You're not supposed to smile unless you want something," he says.

"How do they remember who asked for what, then find them again in the crowd?"

"They serve at their parties too," he says.

Dalzenia holds forth in the kitchen, but Cap'n Smith masterminds the entire operation on our side of the swinging butler's door. An elegant African-American man with graying hair, he's everywhere at once. He balances his silver tray of champagne flutes on one white-gloved hand, proffers linen cocktail napkins with the other. He communicates silently with the legion of servers under him. Do God and the angels work like this?

"Don't they hate us?" I say.

With an ear-splitting crack, the sky breaks open. It's a real Texas thunderstorm; the lightning pops apocalyptically. The guests run inside from the garden. Our ice sculpture washes away in the downpour.

The incoming guests slow to a trickle; the early-arriving guests begin to leave.

"Y'all are so sweet to come," Peaches says to them.

"'Joyed it!" they say.

"That's all you ever need to say to get along with this crowd," Gabriel says to me. "'Perfect,' and 'Joyed it.'"

"Y'all stay here and say 'bye to people, while I get someone to bring you some food," Peaches says.

The second Peaches goes off, King abandons his post.

"Y'all are so sweet to come," we say to several people on their way out. A few late arrivals crash into them.

Peaches loses herself in the crowd she produced and directed. Gabriel and I don't get to eat until the caterers are cleaning up after the party.

"I should help Dalzenia clean up after the caterers, but I'm exhausted," I say, as we stagger upstairs to our rooms. "It's not fair she has to clean up after our fun."

"Fun?" he says. "That party was work."

"Fun work for us. Work work for Dalzenia."

"Colleen," he says. He takes me firmly by the shoulders. "Dalzenia has a stature in the household you don't understand. My parents have always been good to her and they'll continue to provide for her."

"When does she get to retire?" I say. "Where will she go, to a Florida condominium?"

"Do we have to reform the entire social system tonight?" he says. "At least Dalzenia isn't homeless."

"But she's not free," I say. "She doesn't have options."

"She gets paid. She has a place to live. My father bought her a car. She gets health care."

"What about Cap'n Smith and all the servers?" I say. "I guess I'd have to grow up with domestic help the way y'all did to be comfortable with it."

"They're not slaves," he says. "They're consultants."

17

Brides Only Beyond
This Point

"You were supposed to tell me when you were ready to get married," Web calls to say.

"When *I* was ready?" I've been living with Gabriel for nine months and engaged to him for five, but Web just won't give up.

"I'm a better date than I would be a husband," he says, "but in your case I'll make an exception."

"You don't seem to understand."

"We'll discuss it this weekend," he says, "when my ship calls at Galveston."

The closest I came to marrying Web was at a Halloween costume ball. I was the groom in Web's tux, and Web was the bride. He spent hours getting made up. We won first prize in the costume competition. On our way home at two in the morning, we got a flat tire. Web got out to change it in his wedding gown. A policeman stopped to help but saw Web was a man. "Let the bride change it," he said, and roared off on his motorcycle.

"Hurricane Web has been upgraded from a tropical depression to a Category Five," I say when I call Gigi in a panic. "He's gone from moderate to dangerous in the Gulf of Mexico and is about to make landfall."

"Where?"

"Galveston. He says if I don't come talk with him, he'll whirl inland to Houston."

"He'll throw a theme party in the library reference room. He'll wreak havoc in Gabriel's E.R. with shuffleboard and dance contests."

"What should I do?"

"This is Texas," she says. "Head him off at the pass."

Sunday morning after Gabriel has left for the E.R., I get ready to drive to the pier where Web's ship has docked. I put on one of my best new suits, a jade sueded silk from Étui, to show Web how loved and taken care of I look now. Every day I look more like a doctor's wife, or at least his fiancée.

I drive south on I-45; the freeway pulls me along against my will. Out of the city, the sun beats down on the depleted fields. The oil refineries of La Marque and Texas City belch on the horizon. Once over the causeway, there's no turning back. On Galveston Island, I drive past the resort hotel where Web staged the bachelor party at which I was the entertainment, past the jail where I spent the night. In the Silk Stocking district, gaslights burn in front of the Victorian mansions.

When I get to the pier, Web's ship is having a dock party. Poisonous white oleanders sway in the salty breeze. I step into the throng of passengers, who laugh and carouse.

"Surprise!" they shout. They all turn toward me.

A sixteen-piece orchestra bursts into "Here Comes the Bride."

Web descends the gangplank to place an enormous bridal bouquet in my arms. He hasn't changed a bit; handsome and fit in his tux, his dark eyes smolder with mischief. The curlicues of his jet black hair would spin out of control were it not for his barber's sorcery.

I'm dressed for a wedding, but not my own.

Web's kinky friends Gillian and Foster rush up. "I'm your matron of honor," Gillian says.

Web takes my arm. His touch is still electric, but the charge has worn way down.

"Web!" I say. "You can't throw a surprise wedding."

"That's what I love about you," he says. "You're so gullible."

"I don't trust anybody," I say. "How can I when things like this keep happening to me?"

"You mistrust the wrong people," he says.

The guests swim around us, congratulate us. Web hasn't overlooked a single detail. A defrocked priest waits to perform the ceremony. A white carpet runs the length of the dock, set up with chairs. At one end, a table is heaped with gifts, surrounding the wedding cake. Champagne flows from a fountain.

The trouble is, I'm in love with Gabriel.

"Who are they?" I ask Web, of six sirens lined up like wistful bridesmaids.

"The contestants," he says.

I turn away, fling my bouquet at them, over my shoulder. I run back down the dock as if running from pirates. Waves churn below me as I drive back over the causeway, drive back to Houston, to Gabriel.

"Let's go out and celebrate," I say when Gabriel gets home that night.

"Celebrate what?"

"I'll tell you later," I say. "Right now I just want to have some fun."

"Why can't we have fun at home?"

"Let's go dancing," I say. "People with jobs like ours have to make a point of working fun into our schedules."

Gabriel shrugs and picks up his truck keys. He must love me a lot if he's willing to go dancing.

"We're textbook," I say, as we drive downtown on San Jacinto. "A sexually anxious recovering co-dependent from a violent broken home, and a guilty divorced father thrashing around in an emergency room are bound to have problems having fun."

"Those aren't the real categories," he says.

I want to go to Shadow, where neither of us has been, but we can't find it. "It's got to be here somewhere," I say. "It's so in they don't have a sign."

"What type of music do they have?"

"Handbag,"

"Is that like bagpipes?"

"It's high-energy dance music."

"This is a dangerous part of town this late Sunday night," he says.

San Jacinto is one-way, so we cut down a dark side street to circle the block. This is Chance's part of town, of dark warehouses and closed social service agencies. Homeless people lurk in the shadows.

"Is this what we're going to be like when we're married?" I say. "So out of it we can't even find the club, never mind dance there?"

"It's probably closed on Sunday night," he says, as we drive the long deserted block again.

"It's always open," I say. "Just like we work all the time, some people party all the time."

"Who?" he says. "Besides debutantes."

"Web," I say.

He squares his shoulders, stiffens his spine.

"Don't worry," I say. "I just told Web I'd never go back to him, dancing or no dancing."

Gabriel yanks the steering wheel to the right, pulls over to the curb. "Hold on," he says. "You're still in touch with Web?"

"Web's still in touch with *me*," I say.

"You talked with him?"

"I saw him."

"You saw him?"

"I drove all the way to Galveston today to tell him to give it up," I say. "I did it for us."

"That dog won't hunt," he says.

We sit there with the hazard lights on. Pimps and car-jackers cruise by us. Gabriel turns to stone. Just like my mother's silence, Gabriel's doesn't give me anything to refute, any way to defend myself.

"You're still in touch with Felicity," I say after a while.

"We have a child," he says.

Gabriel still has a wife and family. He'll never forgive himself for divorcing Felicity; he'll want to pay for marrying her the rest of his life. Felicity will use his devotion to Gabe to stay in the relationship by fighting with him for the next twenty years, maybe forever. I'd be in the fight but not of it. "I'm a fifth wheel," I say.

"Is there anything else you haven't told me?"

"Dear Abby says I don't have to," I say. "You don't have to tell someone *everything*."

He looks deafened by all the skeletons rattling around in my closet, dying to jump out. The truth is, the more I tell him, the more righteous he becomes and the more depraved I seem. How can I marry someone who makes me feel like that?

When I was sixteen and couldn't decide whether or not to enter the convent, the nuns had me make a list of advantages and disadvantages. On the negative list, Gabriel has Felicity, long hours in the E.R., control issues. Even the positive list of all his good qualities is clouded with my fear of losing him. I know love could wipe out the bad list entirely. My love for Gabriel is here somewhere, but I can't find it through the wall of water behind my eyes.

"I can't marry you," I say, and take off my engagement ring. "You're too serious, too rich—and too Texan."

He puts my ring in his pocket, then turns to fix me in his gaze.

"Too serious?" he says. "I'm working on that. Too rich? Felicity's working on that. But too Texan?" he says, and sits taller in the saddle. "I will always be more Texan than you."

He starts the truck. We get on Fannin, a one-way street out of downtown, drive away from ourselves as fast as we can.

Gabriel gets paged the minute we get home. He calls the hospital. "I have to go in to the E.R.," he says when he hangs up. "A homeless man got shot near the Transco Tower."

"We have to resolve this argument," I say.

We stand there, stare each other down. Our frustration is as perfect as our love once was. When I look at Gabriel and am afraid, I see the full force of my own rage. His pager goes off again. He walks out of the apartment, my engagement ring still in his pocket. He trudges down the stairs, climbs into his pickup, slams the door.

I follow him, helplessly. I peer at him through the window. His face has lost all color, suddenly translucent. His eyes are gray with sadness, enormous with terror, filled with tears. Dark circles under his eyes drag the bottom lids down. Never have I seen him so intimately, so bare. How can I comfort him through the glass? This is his private face. What secret of grief is it he shares only with himself?

He drives off. He doesn't come home that night.

Why is it there are some things you can find out about a man only by fighting with him? I pace all night from room to room. I can't go to Gigi's, she could be pumping up Malcolm. I can't deal with anyone else's neuroses. If I go to a shelter, will I get a pillowcase with a sheet and towel inside? Why is it when you most need somewhere to go, you can't think of a single place?

In the morning, I go downtown to look for Chance. It's been a while since I've heard from him. He told me he stays at the encampment of homeless people next to the convention center. But the homeless people have been evicted, the encampment broken down. Chance said this would happen when the city outlawed aggressive panhandling and the accumulation of human waste.

Across the street, the bridal expo has begun in the convention center. I go in to ask about the encampment. I pass through a turnstile that goes only one way, under an enormous sign that says "Brides Only Beyond This Point." I'm herded down a roped-off chute toward a computer station for Bride's Check-In. I ask the perky clerk the way out, but she misunderstands, enters me on the computer for door-prize drawings for china, flatware, a honeymoon trip. I peel the wax paper back from my Bride-to-Be name tag, then throw the whole thing away.

I can relate to being homeless. To be so tired of holding things together all I can do is let go. To wear rags and wander in the street, looking for a bench and a half-eaten sandwich.

I wander under floral archways, through the crowd of prancing brides and bridesmaids, determined mothers, sheepish grooms. It's a livestock show for brides, aisle after aisle of jewelry, lingerie. Makeup experts snare brides going by. Posters for cosmetic dentistry show before and after pictures of toothy bridal mouths.

"Are you the mother of the bride?" a caterer asks me. His booth is crammed with plastic-coated versions of his dishes.

"No," I say. All the brides are eighteen, even the pregnant ones.

"Good," he says. "I give a discount if the mother's not involved."

"How many does that feed?" brides ask, and point at one towering cake after another. One has frosted letters that read "Time to Hang Up Your Spurs, Jake!"

"Someone's got to explain the Grand March to your guests," a disc jockey says, "and it might as well be me." He hands me a list of all the kinds of music he plays—country and western, ballroom, disco, rap.

"You've got to have wedding-planner software," a vendor says, and thrusts her brochure at me.

I take it to show Gigi. "My bridal software would have to be virtual reality," I say.

Photographers show albums of other people's weddings.

"We have your wedding photos to you the day after," one of them says. "Some people get divorced before their pictures are developed. I tell my photolab, print these up, this marriage isn't going to last."

I turn away to watch a wedding video. It's a made-for-TV movie, with a wild-West theme. The groom pushes the bride's behind into a horse-drawn stagecoach. The wedding party is dressed in period costume that can only be described as saloon. The bridesmaids wear red and black can-can dresses hiked above the knee in the front and ruffled in the back. In church, the bride takes the microphone to sing a Patsy Cline song to the groom. At the reception in the church hall, the guests dance the two-step, western polka, Cotton-Eyed Joe. Someone other than the groom puts his hand down the bride's bodice. The happy couple stuff each other with cake, then the groom pulls off the bride's garter with his teeth. They ride off in the stagecoach; the bride pops her head out to wave to the camera. It ends with a full roll of credits.

I dodge department-store bridal consultants who want to sign me up for instant credit. Pachelbel's Canon in D Major competes with travel agents pushing scuba-diving honeymoons. Mrs. Texas and Mrs. Black Texas are both here in their tiaras.

"It's *my* wedding," a bride says in a loud voice to her groom. They fight over where to have the reception.

Another bride shows her maid of honor the china she selected. "I told Steve he could help with the everyday ware," she says, "but I have the china under control."

A man sits alone at the Father of the Bride Survival Center. There aren't any fathers of the bride in a hundred miles. Next to him, a couple in a waterbed with a breakfast tray advertise a hotel's wedding-night special.

Woozy from the smell of white cake and sugary frosting, I sit down to watch the bridal fashion show—wedding gowns, tuxedos, bridesmaid and flower-girl dresses. Models dance down the runway. After each fashion show, brides-to-be scramble to catch bouquets tossed for prizes. A bouquet lands at my feet. I win a thousand dollars' worth of honeymoon lingerie. Too depressed to collect it, I slip out under a heart-shaped archway of pink and white balloons.

18

Too Dumb to Quit

I drag myself to my self-defense class that evening. I'm ready to quit, even though I've made it to Advanced/Graduating. A woman who graduated long ago drops into our class for a surprise demonstration. She does everything perfectly.

"She can walk and chew gum at the same time," Bubba says. "You can walk," he says to Marcy. "You can chew," he says to Susan. "But none of you can do both."

"I can't walk *or* chew," I say to Gigi. "I did everything right with Gabriel, and look what happened."

"The streets are littered with women who did everything right," she says. "As far as getting married goes, you're hard to place."

"I'm no match for Gabriel and his family."

"They're getting back at you for the Yankees winning the war."

"Maybe getting married isn't such a great idea. What about that song that goes, ' 'Tis a gift to be single.' "

" 'To be *simple*,' " she says. "Not the same thing at all."

"You're right," I say. "Being single is complicated."

"Nobody meets Mr. Right until after she's married, anyway. He's called Mr. Right because you meet him right after it's too late."

"Is it ever too late to meet Mr. Wrong?" I ask.

Now that we've ostensibly learned to fight from the ground, we have to learn to fight standing up and lying down, and put all the techniques together.

"Not only was Gabriel the only man I ever wanted to marry," I tell Gigi while we watch Susan take her turn, "I can't imagine my life without him."

"That's a problem," she says. "Maybe you had a past life together."

"Then even psychotherapy wouldn't help."

"You could go to a hypnotist," she says, "like the one who helped me quit smoking."

"I went to a hypnotist for past-life regression, but my past lives were depressing. Why get depressed about those lives when my present life is depressing enough?"

"How can I support you?" she says, in networking parlance.

"Not in the style to which I've become accustomed."

"At least you won't complicate your networking with a new name," she says. "Everyone in our group has too many names."

"Their own, their husband's, or hyphenated?"

"Then when they get divorced, they take back their maiden names. By the time they remarry, they've got too many I.D.'s and are ambivalent besides. Everyone knows everyone by a different name, depending on what they were going through when they met."

"I'm so out of step," I say. "Everyone's getting divorced for the second or third time and I just broke off my first engagement."

"Worse, everyone's now related to everyone else by a series of divorces."

"We're going to have a good fight," Bubba says when it's my turn.

I refuse to adjust on any level to losing Gabriel. "Stay back!" I say. My heart pounds so hard my sweatshirt throbs in and out. My kick connects, but he keeps coming. I knee him and strike with my arms, but he wins.

"At least you didn't go ahead and marry Web," Gigi says. "It would've been just like you to do the final stupid thing."

"I'm used to losing men," I say. "It's the only relationship thing I'm good at."

"The Queen told Prince Charles and Princess Di to get a divorce."

"My family shadow notwithstanding," I say, "my sexual relationship with Gabriel could have been saved."

"Malcolm still can't get it up, but I'm consorting with my vibrator."

"Aren't you afraid once you get used to it nothing else will work?"

"People have been using various devices for thousands of years—look at the Japanese."

"The Japanese probably make a good vibrator," I say. "But it doesn't seem natural."

"You have this idea in your head there's a right way to do things you have to spend the rest of your life learning."

"Isn't there?"

"In sex, Colleen," she says, *"there's no right way."*

Bubba starts slipping our kicks by turning sideways at the last moment. "Most muggers won't know to slip a kick," he says. "But there'll be the one that will. You got to square off, come at him with your knees to his chest. Boom! Boom! Boom!"

If we're not on him quickly enough, he pushes us down

and we're in for a ground fight, with all those techniques to remember. The worse I am, the worse I get.

"I know what your problem is," Bubba says when I fail to leap into him. "You don't want to get hurt."

Enraged, nothing left to lose, I throw myself into our next fight. My lip swells when I bang it on his helmet. I tear up my ring finger yanking him toward me.

"Okay, girls, pick it up," Bubba says in disgust.

I drag away my mat. "Is anybody really happy?" I ask Gigi.

"The people in the Lands' End catalog."

"Gabriel's onto something, obsessing over catalogs."

"If you did that," she says, "you'd be the only unhappy person wearing Lands' End clothes."

"I'm happy when I've organized my closet."

"It gives you the illusion of having control over your life."

"When my closet is organized," I say, "I don't care whether I have control over my life or not."

"How will we know when we're ready to graduate?" Barbara asks Bubba.

"*I'll* know," he says. He paces back and forth. "When I don't want to attack you anymore, when I don't want to take the punishment."

It's incredible to me our puny kicks and punches could have any effect on him through all that padding. Nevertheless, the strap on his chestplate keeps breaking. His duct tape is peeling off all over, and the stuffing inside is unraveling.

"Will anyone from our class graduate soon?" I ask Bubba after the others have left. I can relate to the despair of children who don't do well in school, of the homeless who can't work within the system My mind is slow, but my body is days behind my mind, unable to do what my mind tells it until it's too late. I feel bruises on my bruises.

Bubba peels off his padded chestplate. "Nah," he says. "Those other girls may never come back. I know why, too. They're afraid of the graduation test, but I set it up to be frightening. This whole course is supposed to be frightening."

"It is that."

"Months from now I'll run into them at the supermarket or someplace," he goes on. "They'll duck like they don't even know me."

"I won't leave until I graduate," I say. "But this is hard for me."

"Then you've got courage." He takes off his helmet, looks me in the eye. He looks drawn and exhausted, his dark hair matted with sweat. "People see me in a martial arts competition and they think I'm a natural, that it comes easy." He unzips his camouflage jumpsuit, pulls out great wads of padding, foam, cloth, cardboard. He steps out of the suit. "But the truth is, I practiced until I got it right. I was too dumb to quit."

I stare at Bubba in his sweatpants and sweatshirt, like me. He looks vulnerable, even kind.

"Too dumb to quit?"

"Ice that lip down," he says.

He stuffs all his protective equipment into two enormous duffel bags, then, hunched over with the weight of them, limps out of the gym.

Too dumb to quit. I embrace this revelation like a mantra. Walking home, I look for a mugger to practice on, but birds pierce the soft night with sweetness. Golden squares of windows light the way from house to house.

One of the principles of networking is you're never further

than five contacts away from anything you want. Gigi sold an anti-viral software package to a marketing strategist whose ropes course facilitator is married to the former sister-in-law of the executive editor of the *New England Journal of Medicine*. That's how I managed to place the only personal ever in the *New England Journal:* "Yankee seeks Texan. Must be E.R. doc, love sports catalogs, and come with two-year-old son from previous marriage." I faxed it months ago, before Gabriel and I were engaged, never mind disengaged.

Gabriel sits in his chair reading the *New England Journal of Medicine* when I walk in. "Yankee seeks Texan?" he says.

"Yankee *loves* Texan," I say.

"Texan loves Yankee." He stands up, his arms at his sides like a gorilla badly in need of a hug.

He has filled the condo with aromatherapy votive candles. They light up the living room and dining alcove, the kitchen and hallway, glow in a trail to the bedroom. I hope he read the instructions and chose aphrodisiac candles rather than those for constipation or insomnia.

"Where have you been?" I say.

"The E.R. nurse and I spent last night in intensive care," he says.

"So there is someone else?"

"No way," he says. "We were overcome by fumes from a patient who committed suicide by dousing herself with a pesticide. When we didn't revive on gurneys in the parking lot, we went on ventilators."

I can't help it, I walk into his arms. "How are you now?"

"Better, home with you," he says. "I hoped and prayed you hadn't left me."

"I tried, but you weren't here to leave."

"Then passing out was worth it." He tries to kiss me but my lip is still too puffy. He takes my hand to kiss, but my empty ring finger is too swollen and bruised to touch.

"What happened?" he says, and searches my face. "You look like you've been rode hard and put up wet."

"I got hurt in self-defense."

"Sorry I wasn't around when you needed me."

"I was a good person not to be around."

"We're going to the E.R. right now." He picks up the keys to his truck and wraps his doctor's coat around my shoulders.

"You're exhausted," I say. "I'll go tomorrow."

"Keep it elevated to hold down the swelling." He wraps my finger in a splint he improvises out of ice cubes in a dish towel. From his pickup phone, he calls an orthopedist to meet us at the E.R. "She doesn't have any upward mobility," he tells him, "but her sensation seems okay."

He looks over at me several times on our drive to the hospital.

"I grew up with a distorted sense of a man's emotional makeup," I say.

He puts his arm around me. "While I was on the ventilator," he says after a while, "I let go of a lot of stuff."

"What was it?"

"I don't know," he says. "It's all gone."

We sit down in the hall outside the orthopedist's examination room.

A nurse ushers me into the doctor's tiny room. "Dr. Mills will be with you in a minute," she says. "Sit here—you're sitting on his stool."

I've been living with a doctor less than a year and already I act like I own the place.

Gabriel says orthopods used to be big burly surgeons who could wield saws and drills, but now anyone can handle the power tools. Dr. Mills is young and bony. It takes him just a second to decide I need an x-ray.

"Please get up on the table," the technician in X-ray says. "You're not preguant, are you?"

"I hope not," I say.

She takes pictures of my finger from several angles. I wait on a bench with a dozen other people.

The technician rushes out, waving my x-rays in a folder. "Ms. Sweeney!" she says. "Remind me never to take self-defense!"

I wait for Dr. Mills in his office and worry how bad this could turn out to be. I've learned from Gabriel a person could be sitting here like this one minute, and the next be wheeled into surgery for a hand removal.

"Fractured," Dr. Mills says. He frowns at me. He tapes my finger and puts it in a splint. "It's never going to be perfect, but it'll probably be all right."

Gabriel sits cross-legged, asleep from exhaustion, on the floor outside Dr. Mills's office. The circles under his eyes are deep, his cheeks pale above his beard. Even in sleep he's dignified, not slack-jawed and snoring like most men. He's in silent repose, as if meditating deeply.

"I'm sorry," I say. I wake him up as gently as I can.

"Sorry I'm not always emotionally available," he says on the drive home. "Sometimes the emotions available to me aren't the ones I want."

"I'm a hard person to be emotionally available to."

"We could be emotionally unavailable together."

I look at him, he looks at me. No one but Gabriel has ever looked at me with that much love.

"What's our elevation?" I say. It's the next best thing to knowing what time we have our second nanosecond.

Gabriel studies his altimeter watch, does higher mathematics in his head.

"Doesn't your watch just tell you outright?" I say.

"I set it one thousand and two hundred forty-six feet higher because the Houston underpasses make it read lower than sea level," he says. He takes a deep breath. "Will you marry me for sure?"

We begin our lovemaking way out here, at the edges of our defenses. We undress each other in an urgent chaos of hands, fingers, buttons, cloth. We drop the shapes of our silhouettes.

I step out of my clothes into air as cool as water. I'm weightless without them, layer upon layer of cotton and silk. Without these to hold me together, my very limbs unknit. I'm loose inside, with pockets of air.

"It's just me," he says, when I look again into his eyes.

I'm going to be married to Gabriel. My parents were married. I swim past visions of them, naked and fighting, and wonder how long I've been swimming.

Outside, it's raining. Hard drops spatter the windows, pelt the concrete balcony. Traffic washes up and down the street. An airplane drones overhead, sinks more deeply into the wet night sky.

I swim and swim until, with Gabriel, I'm filled with sweetness so subtle it permeates my bones.

Car tires suck the pavement; a door closes with a muffled slam. A child calls out to a woman; a woman calls out to a man. A telephone rings softly in the next apartment. These become sexual sounds, pervading our secret space. They become sex in its very nature, and love itself.

19

The Stepmothering Hormone

"Girlfriend," Vanessa says, "your homeless game is over."

While I was at the bridal exposition, a homeless veteran held eight hostages at gunpoint in the library Reference Room. He called Houston's top country-and-western radio station from the Reference Room phone to say he'd been wronged by the government.

"This proves how urgently the homeless need library services," I say.

"We'll never get them to follow the rules," she says. "The trustees voted to spend your project money on metal detectors instead."

The homeless don't follow society's rules because they don't trust society, with good reason. Chance says that society needs the homeless to carry those parts of itself it hides. It needs them to be bad so it can go on thinking of itself as good.

"Putting in metal detectors now is like locking the barn door after the cows got out," I say.

"After the *horse* got out," she says. "If you're going to stay in Texas, you'd better get your ranch animals straight."

"How do the trustees suggest the library address the roots of our social problems?"

"They want the library collection purged of materials that reinforce negative stereotypes," she says. "Books about singing Negro cotton pickers, girls fulfilled by housework, that sort of thing."

"I suppose you want me to do it," I say, "but destroying evidence won't solve the problems."

"They want a person of color to purge the collection," she says, *sotto voce*.

"But I'm qualified otherwise."

"You'd have to prove yourself," she says. "Always be neat and clean, never be late for work. Don't abuse your library key to steal the computer equipment."

"Vanessa!" I say.

"The trustees don't trust white people," she says. "I'm sorry, that's just the way it is."

I see myself chained to the stacks. "Who freed the hostages?"

"Ralph, the bookmobile librarian."

"But Ralph's a wuss!"

"Not anymore," she says. "He saved two librarians and six patrons, and the trustees are buying him a new bookmobile."

"Will his bookmobile drive to homeless encampments?"

"That homeless dude didn't want library service," she says. "He wanted a pardon from the president."

"What for?"

"He didn't say."

"The library could have made a difference to so many homeless people if that man hadn't ruined it for everybody."

"Don't feel badly about it, girl," Vanessa says. "There are assholes even among the oppressed."

"I have only one more shelter to visit to complete my study."

She sighs. "Do it, then send your whole proposal to document storage."

"But that's oblivion."

"Someone will find it after the Apocalypse," she says.

When I asked my mother where she met my father, she said at a U.S.O. U.F.O., I thought she said, but it was at a U.S. Officer's club dance. They might as well have come from different planets.

I've put off the most heartbreaking homeless group for last—undocumented aliens. *Aliens* makes it sound as if they got off a U.F.O., instead of walking all the way from the border of Mexico—Hondurans, Guatemalans, Peruvians, Chileans, Costa Ricans.

I wedge my VW into a parking place among the abandoned cars and beat-up pickups that hug the ditches along the road. The shelter is shabby but clean, with cast-off furniture, unpainted cinder-block rooms. The telephone rings. Children run and screech in several languages and dialects. No one speaks English at this shelter; it doesn't even have a name. I'm reduced to wordlessness, no need for any pretense at questions now.

Women and children bend over a mound of clothes in the center of the largest room. They hold out-of-style dresses, stretched-out underwear, frayed shirts up to themselves and search for something better than the rags they wear.

"This is clothing day," Matt Stevens, the shelter director tells me. He speaks simply, so used to talking with refugees in their own languages that his native English is tinged with an accent. "They get what won't sell in our thrift shop next door."

I hover at the edge of the room. The walls are bare except for fourteen white paper crosses pasted to them. "Are those the Stations of the Cross?" I say.

"You know about the Stations?" Matt says.

Even as they begin to pick up the pieces of their lives, the homeless keep coming to terms with loss. If we could answer the loss question, library service would take care of itself.

"At any given time, we have up to a hundred refugees—men, women, and children," Matt says, "although we've sometimes had many more, using all the beds and every inch of floor space. We also house undocumented battered women, since the other shelters can't help them. We guarantee they won't have to go back to their batterers."

"Why do they come to the U.S.?"

"To escape the poverty they suffered in their countries," he says. "So many lost relatives in the war. Bad as things are, they have hope here; all they had there was despair."

"Where do you get your funds?"

"From our thrift shop and donations from individuals and churches," he says. "We don't have salaries—our staff are young people who want to serve the poor. We believe individuals rather than the government are personally responsible for helping the poor. It's at least an attempt to challenge the materialism of our culture."

"How could the library help?" I ask.

"In any way that would address the problems of unemployment, language, literacy, resources for training," he says. "Having a job's the most important thing, to support their families, to live like human beings. These are hard-working people. People like us can help them over the hump."

"How do you cope, day after day?"

"It's very hard," he says, "the fatigue. Faith and prayer carry us through."

Children run by and shriek with laughter.

"Buenos dias," he says to the tired mothers chasing after them.

I leave, then look despondently into the shelter's adjacent thrift shop. Among the racks crammed with drab out-of-season clothes stands a mannequin, serene as an angel. She wears the most gorgeous wedding gown I've ever seen— white silk shantung and French Alençon lace. Delicate lace scallops trim the off-the-shoulder sweetheart neckline. The fitted bodice is elaborately embroidered with swirling pearls. The long, full skirt falls in graceful folds from a dropped basque waist. What takes my breath away is the tiara adorned with pearls and white silk rosebuds—a crown for the veil, a waterfall of white lace cascading to the floor. It's all real—real silk, real lace.

"It comes with a long cathedral train," the saleswoman says. She's a tiny Latina, ancient and wizened.

The gown fits me so perfectly, my eyes fill when I see myself in the thrift shop mirror. I feel like a debutante, bride, crowned queen all in one. "How much does it cost?" I say.

"Can you afford seventy-five dollars?" she says. "It's a donation to the shelter."

"I can afford two hundred."

"Most people who come in here can't afford nothing," she says.

Gabriel and I rush around late one Friday afternoon to pick up our marriage license, my shoes, Gabriel's tails, the invitations, our wedding rings. Friday rush-hour traffic is the worst; bumper-to-bumper cars and trucks move just fast enough to be dangerous. No one is ever in the lane he or she wants to be. Vehicles entering the freeway slide left three lanes so as not to be forced off at the upcoming exits, crossing traffic with those in the fast lanes hurtling sideways to exit right.

He won't tell me where we're going on our honeymoon.

"How do I know what to pack?" I say.

"Just bring your personal things," he says. "I told Gigi where we're going and she's buying your honeymoon wardrobe on my credit card."

"Wait until you see your bill."

Felicity insists that if Gabriel wants to see Gabe this weekend, he has to pick him up Friday evening instead of Saturday morning.

"If you wanted Gabe Friday evening, she'd make you wait until Saturday," I say.

"I know."

"Why does she want to get back at you when *she* filed for divorce?"

"I'd ask for a pardon," he says, "if I knew what to be pardoned for."

"Our mistakes aren't the end of the world."

"Someone's responsible."

"We have to recycle more," I say. "We have to believe that the good we do in the world outweighs the bad."

Other drivers catch my eye as I watch for space in the next lane. Their kindness is all the more piercing for the danger.

"Do you still feel like a fifth wheel?" Gabriel says.

"We had a recount," I say. "I'm the fourth counting you, Gabe, and Felicity. The pickup won't run without me."

After our errands, we pick up Gabe at his Montessori school.

"Colleen and I are getting married, Gabe," Gabriel says.

"You're stuck with me forever," I tell him. "But your parents and I are going to pull together."

Tuckered out from his day, he's asleep by the time we

drive into the parking lot of God's Country Club. Gabriel tenderly unfastens his car seat belt, but Gabe doesn't stir.

"I'll go up and unroll his sleeping bag," Gabriel says, "then carry him up and tuck him in." He unloads our wedding things from the back of the pickup, lugs them all up the stairs.

I watch Gabe sleep, feel the stepmothering hormone begin to kick in. His little-boy skin is smooth in repose, his cheeks pink and round, his eyelids almost translucent over his closed eyes.

I did everything anyone ever asked of me in the hope of being loved. Gabe, on the other hand, is so loved wherever he goes—by his mother, his father, his teachers—that being lovable is never in question. He digs in his heels if cajoled; he can afford to question motives. I vow never to cajole Gabe. My father spoke to manipulate me, my mother as if I were her administrative assistant. It was a job, being my mother's child. But I know now my parents loved me all along.

I climb out of the pickup.

The air falls suddenly still. I hold my breath to listen. Someone moves in the shadows.

"Stay back!" I say.

But the man skulks toward Gabe and me. Almost paralyzed with fear, I raise my knee in slow motion, extend my leg in a horrible ballet. He looks charred; in his eyes I see more pain than I can stand—they're black with it, clouded with grief. He stares back. Stay back, don't go, don't stay: be still. So close to my fear, but what am I afraid of? That my father will kill my mother, but she isn't dead, only quiet. That they'll abandon me, but they've only exiled themselves, homeless on a planet so small that no exile is possible. That by marrying Gabriel I'll live out my parents' marriage, taking one part then the other, over and over, day in and day out. I'm tired of being afraid. Nothing, good or bad, exists outside myself that doesn't exist inside as well.

The man drops his gaze. He backs away into the darkness, disappears. I stand there, shake with the impossibility of reconciling my need to defend with my terror of defending, my need to love with my terror of loving. Is the world the sum total of all our choices to love or be afraid?

Gabe climbs out of his car seat, wide-eyed and sleepy. He rubs his eyes with his little fists. He turns to me with his blue gaze, breaks into a trusting smile. I hold him tightly in my arms. He feels soft yet solid, sturdy as he clasps his little arms around my neck. I feel his warm, moist breath as he nestles his face into my shoulder.

Gabriel reappears, looks at me, puzzled.

"I just graduated from my self-defense course," I say.

He reaches for Gabe, but Gabe wants to walk up the stairs himself. He takes one of my hands and one of Gabriel's. Together we walk slowly up the stairs.

20

Two Thongs Don't
Make a Right

Gigi picks me up for my bachelorette party on a sultry evening in early spring, the air heavy with honeysuckle and jasmine. I have no idea where we're going until she pulls up to Bad Boy, Houston's hottest women's club with male dancers. The valet flies out the front door in tuxedo pants and black bow tie to open the car door for me. Shirtless, he embraces me with his pecs.

A big "Private Party" sign is posted inside the door. Well-dressed women swarm around nearly naked men dancing on three separate stages.

"We can't go in, Gigi," I say. "Someone's having a party."

"That's us! Our networking group took over the club."

"They're not in our group," I say of three frightened men cowering behind the cashier.

"We don't allow men in as customers," the cashier says. "These guys are here for the midnight amateur competition—with crowds this tough, we do auditions."

The air is thick with estrogen. I accustom my eyes to the darkness, strobe lights flashing like bursting bombs. The club is furnished in dark velvets, chairs upholstered deep purple, black tables shiny as patent leather. The long, sleek bar glitters with green and amber bottles. Light glows like small rubies in goblets of red wine.

"Are all your members over twenty-one?" the cashier, who looks barely twenty-one herself, asks Gigi.

"Try over forty-one," Gigi says.

"We're only over thirty-one," I say.

"Some are over sixty-one," Gigi says.

"Do you keep people out for being too old?" I ask the cashier. I'd be mortified if some of Houston's top women executives couldn't get into my bachelorette party.

"Congratulations, Colleen!" everyone says. They air-kiss as we pass through the crowd. The women network like crazy, occasionally eyeing the dancing men to size them up as potential clients.

"My bank would float these gorgeous boys low-interest loans until they got real jobs," Barbara says.

"Don't kid yourself," Marcy, a C.P.A., says. "They're all in the top tax bracket."

Gigi has reserved a table for us right in front of the center stage, with Barbara, Marcy, and Susan. I guess if I got through self-defense with them, I can make it through this. The stage is two feet high, the dancer's bulging crotch at eye level. I try not to look.

"Don't worry," Gigi says. "They won't get too gross because they know women don't go for that like men do."

"Speak for yourself," Barbara says.

Gigi orders champagne.

Our waiter is back in a New York second dressed like the valet in tuxedo pants, pecs, black tie. "Did you miss me?" he says. He flashes an ingratiating grin.

"*I* did," Barbara says.

Stripped of body hair, the waiters and dancers seem more naked than naked. Some have elegant *GQ* hairstyles; others have long, wild manes that make them look as if they've stepped off the cover of a romance novel. The side-stage dancers wear nothing but butt-thongs, and leather boots up to their knees.

Above us on the center stage, a man comes out in a silver satin pajama-and-robe ensemble he tantalizingly dances off, piece by piece. When he's down to his thong, he turns around so we can ogle him. He flexes one buttock at a time, then turns front to flex one pec at a time.

"What else do you think he can wiggle?" Barbara says.

"His ears, I hope," I say.

Barbara leans over to tuck a dollar bill into his thong strap. He grins at her, then dances off the stage. After him, we get a cowboy in chaps, a businessman with a whip, a musclebound construction worker, and a Marine.

"They're playing to our fantasies!" Gigi says.

The Marine strips off his jacket, pants, shirt in pulsating rhythm to the disco music. He struts around the stage in his hat, his biceps and thigh muscles rippling.

"No way does a Marine wear an iridescent thong like that," I say.

"Their outfits are write-offs, for sure," Marcy says.

"Even their thongs?" I say.

"Especially."

Their thongs must cost a lot. There's not much up the back, but the fronts are like long shiny socks in neon green, orange, pink, covered with sequins and glitter.

"Don't you love how they glow in the dark?" Barbara says.

We don't answer; we're mesmerized.

"This isn't like the old days when the guys wore jock straps," Marcy says. "They were so bunched up you couldn't tell what they had."

"These guys put a golf ball in the bottom of the thong to weigh it down and make it swing like that," Gigi says.

"More likely a tennis ball," Barbara says.

Susan looks as if she just learned there is no Santa. "Someone has to feel it to find out," she says.

"You do it, Colleen," they all say, and turn toward me. "It's your bachelorette party."

"I think not," I say.

"We can sue if it's fake," Susan says. "We're entitled to Truth in Erections."

"Wouldn't a real erection stick out instead of hanging like that?" I say.

Erections having come up, Gigi tells us the whole story of how she dumped Malcolm because she got tired of his neurosing over his impotence. "I feel like someone just let me out of jail," she says. "After the pump didn't work out, he tried injections. I didn't mind that nothing was still happening, but why did he have to wake me up to tell me?"

We all murmur and empathize supportively.

"Did you give back his presents?" I ask. He gave her lots of jewelry—diamond tennis bracelets, watches, rings.

"I insisted I give them back and he insisted I keep them," she says. "He won."

"He might think he still has a claim on you," Barbara says.

"I already have a new man," she says, "an airline pilot I met during a layover in St. Louis. He flew in to be with me last night."

"Already?" I say.

"We didn't do anything," she says.

"Then why'd he sleep over?" I say.

"That's very in now," she says.

Engaged for such a short time, I'm already falling behind on trends.

"When you're married you'll really be out of it," Marcy says, "but it will matter less."

"How did you meet your husband?" Barbara asks Marcy.

"He applied for a job at my accounting firm," she says. "I fell in love with him on his resume and proposed at his interview. He decided he'd rather have me for a wife than a boss."

Women line up at each of the three stages to wait their turns to slip crisp bills into the thong straps. The Marine's strap flaps with folded bills.

"Look at all that unreported tip income," Marcy says, and whistles. "He needs my help to figure his FICA."

We watch while Liz, an otolaryngologist, tucks her business card in his G-string. "This music is very bad for your hearing," she shouts to him above the pulsing disco.

Barbara gets in line. When it's her turn, she slips a bill under the Marine's thong strap, then slowly rubs her palms up and down his thighs.

Our eyes collectively widen.

"How much do you suppose that set her back?" Gigi says.

"Had to be at least a ten," Marcy says.

The Marine leans over to hear what Barbara whispers in his ear. Barbara slips another bill under his strap.

"She's doing it again!" Gigi says.

"He likes Barbara," I say. "His tennis ball just got heavier."

Barbara comes back to her seat, sits down with a smug smile. The rest of us are too jealous to talk to her.

We turn to watch Elissa, president of a multinational corporation, whip the dancer on a side-stage with her long red hair. Our fellow networkers clap and urge her on. The disc jockey stops the music. Elissa and the dancer are having a wonderful time, but the d.j. won't start the music again until she stops.

"They're afraid we'll get out of control!" Susan says.

Elissa's dancer settles for taking her delicate hands and stroking his chest and inner thighs with them.

"She must be expensing this," Marcy says.

The lines in front of each of the stages are now ten women deep. Some of the women kiss the men; others run their hands over their chests and buttocks. Most just talk while the men listen.

"In men's clubs, the men never want to talk to the women," Gigi says.

"This proves men will listen to women if you pay them enough," Marcy says.

"Psychotherapists have known that for years," Susan says.

"What do you talk about to these guys?" Gigi says. "It's not covered in my business protocol book."

"Why don't you go ask one?" I say. "There's an airline pilot for you."

We all turn back to the center stage, where a dancer in a black pilot's uniform unbuttons his brass as he lip-syncs.

"I like my airline pilots home in bed," Gigi says.

"It's the Bad Boy himself," the d.j. announces, as the pilot unbuckles his belt, drops trou.

Women run from the other two lines to get in his.

"This is what comes of traveling too much for our jobs," Marcy says.

"This guy kisses everybody," Barbara says. "I kissed him when he was a Marine."

"Did you think he was going to be faithful?" Gigi asks her.

"He likes it better than the other guys," I say.

"How do you suppose they decide what favors to impart to whom for how much money?" Marcy says.

"They have a sliding scale, depending on your need and their mood," Susan says. She's a psychotherapist.

"What type of referrals do you get?" I ask her.

"People who've lost documents in their computers," she says. "Gigi sends me lots of them."

I gaze around the room. "This is the biggest turnout our networking group has ever had," I say.

"The only one who regretted was Vanessa," Gigi says. "She was called suddenly to Washington to interview for the Librarian of Congress job."

A dancer throws his leg over the president of Barbara's bank.

"I have to go to the ladies' room but I'm afraid I'll miss something!" Barbara says.

"The only reason this works is because we don't have to deal with these guys as real people," I say.

"Fear of intimacy," Susan says. "Need for control."

"Plus, it's fun," Barbara says.

"It's an antidote to our Puritan work ethic and sexual repression," I say.

"Okay," Gigi says to me, "what were you and Gabriel doing last night at this time?"

I look at my watch. It's eleven-thirty. "We were in bed," I say.

Everyone leans in. "Yes?"

"Gabriel got up to move the refrigerator because I heard a drip under it."

"You're wasting a good man," Barbara says. "You should have called a plumber."

"In the middle of the night?" Marcy says. "Marry the man who'll move the refrigerator."

"I'd rather marry a sex object," Barbara says.

"What you need is a sex object who'll move the refrigerator," Susan says.

"Gabriel moved the refrigerator naked," I say, "then we made love."

Everyone sits back with a sigh of relief. We turn our attention back to our musclebound dancer, who looks as if he could move a refrigerator but wouldn't. I don't do refrigerators, he'd say.

"Exhibitionism is making a comeback in this day of safe sex," Susan says.

"Doesn't he make you want to touch?" Barbara says. She cocks her head toward the airline pilot.

We contemplate him. He's perfect all over. The front of his black thong hangs down ten inches.

He picks up on our rapt attention. "Y'all let me know when you're ready for a table dance, hear?" he calls to us.

"Yes!" everyone else at our table says. They look at each other, then at me.

The airline pilot disappears backstage and reappears at our table, stripped of his miniskirt of dollar bills. Although he wears his black thong over a white one, his tennis ball pulls them both down to show more of his lower abdomen than I'm happy with.

"Two thongs don't make a right," I say.

He flies onto the table, the space cleared of drinks and purses. From his ankles up, he courses with musical desire.

My view is such that I feel like the girl who now knows more about penguins than she ever wanted to know. He smiles down at me. He looks dreamily, sleepily deep into my eyes.

It's like having Michelangelo's *David* dance for you, only better. He comes down from the table, and dances suggestively between it and me, so close I melt into the lovely heat of his body. Fragrant waves of musk and almond French milled soap steam from his smooth, lightly bronzed skin. I try to calm my beating heart by reminding myself that our culture has such rituals in place to support one's safe passage from singlehood to wifehood. Margaret Mead has probably done a study of it; tomorrow I'll check the book out of the library.

His dance becomes progressively more provocative. He's leading up to something that's making me very nervous. Even the women who never stopped networking sense his desire; the crowd grows around our table. Cellular phones ring, but nobody answers them. When the tension mounts so high we can hardly stand it, he drops to his knees, puts his hands on my hips, leans in and offers me his—ear.

"What do women talk to you about?" I whisper. "A friend of mine wants to know."

"This is a very kinky crowd," he says. His lips nibble and graze my ear.

"Your sex life?" I ask.

"Marketing strategy," he says. He kisses me gently on the lips.

I draw back; the crowd goes wild.

"How was it?" everyone asks when he dances seductively away.

"It wasn't altogether an unpleasant experience."

The truth is, I don't think I can make it through the amateur contest. Our networking group is still going strong. Some women are banging their Ferragamos on the tables. Others are making the most of the action to cut lucrative business deals. One is selling an insurance policy to the bartender.

"Go home before it's too late," I say to the three male contestants as Gigi and I slip out the door.

The valet looks clear through me to the bottom of my soul. "Don't y'all be strangers now," he says. He lifts me up and puts me into the car.

21

Who Was She?

Gabriel and I marry on the Saturday afternoon after Dr. Mills removes my ring-finger splint. It's early April, the height of wildflower time. Wildflowers—bluebonnets, red Indian paintbrush, yellow buttercups—are to spring in Texas what foliage is to autumn in New England.

That morning, Felicity's phone call wakes me up. Gabriel is already in the shower because he has to pick up Gabe at seven. Gabe is our ring bearer.

"Gabe woke up this morning with a terrible case of jock itch," Felicity says.

I don't know quite what to say.

"He'll scratch the whole way down the aisle," she says.

"Why does she have to tell me about it?" I ask Gabriel as soon as he's out of the shower. "Why couldn't she wait to tell you when you pick him up?"

"Gabe doesn't have jock itch," he says.

A cool breeze blows through the leafy, sun-dappled trees. Our wedding is at the interfaith chapel at Gabriel's hospital, across the courtyard from the emergency room. It's airy and bright, the white walls curving to an arch at the top. Stained glass windows color the sunlight deep red and royal blue. The sanctuary blooms with armloads of bluebonnets and Indian paintbrush. Peaches has seen to it that white ribbons and bows bedeck the pews for family.

"How do you feel?" Gigi says when we meet to get dressed in the tiny room below the chapel foyer. We don't want Gabriel to see me in my wedding gown until I walk down the aisle.

"Like Superwoman," I say. "Able to leap tall class divisions in a single bound."

"Has Gabriel come to terms with your family?"

"He doesn't mind what family I'm from, as long as I marry him from it."

"Did you know we could lose our looks in just one day?" she says as she works on my makeup.

"It happens over time."

"*One day*," she says. "I read it in a magazine."

"Was it a plastic surgery ad?"

Gigi hasn't recovered from my finding such a bridal gown in a shelter thrift shop. "You're dressed for excess," she says, "but you should have gotten married in the eighties, when this dress was in style."

"I'm getting married in the nineties," I say, unruffled, "when Gabriel came on the market."

Arranging my hair under my tiara and veil takes as long as it would to prepare for Houston's Hair Ball. "I have to be really beautiful, if just for today," I say.

"It doesn't matter if you're not the most beautiful woman in the room when you're with the most beautiful man," she says.

My family are all at the church except my father. No one

knows where he is. We know he's in Houston, because my family came from Boston on the same flight, although my father sat in the back of the plane. He's staying at a cheaper motel, because my mother doesn't want to run into him more than necessary.

Doug paid for our father's air ticket, and I paid for his motel, because he's still broke. Doug's trying to sell the house my father inherited from Hazel, to pay off the taxes and debts and rent my father a small apartment. In the meantime, my father lives in it, in the style to which he has long been accustomed.

Peaches and my mother come down to the dressing room in their corsages of cymbidium orchids, their bright dresses miraculously complementary. Peaches is in a dither about who'll walk me down the aisle if my father doesn't show up—a quantum leap above her most challenging seating arrangement. She suggests King; my mother suggests Doug.

"Your mother should walk you down the aisle, as a feminist statement," Gigi says. "Everyone in our networking group would be proud."

"It's just like your father not to show up for your wedding," my mother says.

We hear the rumble of the guests arriving overhead.

"We'll wait for you upstairs in the foyer," Peaches says. "By the time you get there, we'll have made up your mind."

"I've already decided I'll walk myself down the aisle," I tell Gigi after the two mothers get on the tiny elevator.

"Nobody could run home to either of your mothers."

"I'd run home to his and he'd run home to mine."

"You could have a difficult marriage."

"Beats the heck out of a life of difficult affairs."

The elevator comes back down, but Gigi and I can't both

get on with my wedding gown. I send Gigi up ahead to tell the two mothers to chill out. "That's what a maid of honor is for," I say.

She hugs me, steps on the elevator, then turns suddenly to gaze at me. She smiles.

"How do I look?" I ask.

"Flabbergasted."

"Married is something I thought I'd never get," I say.

When the elevator comes back down empty, my gown and I get on. It's so slow I can hardly tell it's moving. To my horror, between the two floors, it comes to a spongy stop. Claustrophobic, I reason with myself that everyone knows I'm in here. Where else could I be?

Several minutes later, I'm convinced there's a power outage. Is a gang crashing the wedding, having shot out the elevator panel in the foyer so no one can escape? Are they robbing all the guests, stealing Peaches's diamonds and my mother's only jewelry? What if Gabriel gets shot, even killed? Are they kidnapping Gabe? I'd faint, but I can't move in my dress. I push all the buttons and the alarm. Nothing happens.

Gabriel will think I'm standing him up at the altar. Everyone will go home; I'll never get married. I'd cry, but I'd ruin my makeup. Worst of all, Gabriel will think I don't love him.

Inexplicably, the elevator starts moving again. The time I was stuck in the elevator was the time my father needed to make it to the chapel. My mother has been escorted to her seat within the ribbon, but Peaches stands in the foyer arguing with a homeless man in baggy brown pants, a worn tweed sportcoat.

"This person insists he's your father," Peaches says to me as I step out of the elevator.

"Hi, Dad," I say. What means more—what people think, or my love for my father, misguided though that may be? I pin a white carnation boutonniere on his worn lapel.

He breaks into his broad, unshaven smile. "Hi, honey," he says. "You look grand."

Peaches allows King to drag her off to her pew. Gigi is poised, ready to go. Gabe is a paragon of good behavior. In his little blue Eton suit with short pants and knee socks, he patiently bears the rings pinned on a Texas-shaped satin pillow. Gabriel is somewhere in the wings at the front of the church.

"Where were you?" I say to my father.

"It was a longer walk from my motel to the chapel than I thought," he says.

"You walked?" I say.

"I'm used to walking," he says, "but this medical center is huge."

The processional music starts, the Trumpet Voluntary. Gabriel wouldn't agree to it at first because he thought I said Strumpet Voluntary. He enters the sanctuary now, followed by King, his best man. They're both dashing in black coats, striped gray trousers, striped black and white four-in-hand ties.

"Go to Daddy," I say to Gabe, "but don't run."

Gabe starts down the aisle. He carries the satin pillow as if delivering a pizza.

"I didn't think to give you money for a taxi," I say to my father. "I'll make sure you have cash for lunch tomorrow before you fly home."

Gigi follows Gabe, now halfway down the aisle. In an opulent blue gown, she carries a bouquet of bluebonnets and gardenias.

"Right next to my motel is a chicken place with a lunch special," my father says. "Two pieces of chicken and one roll for a dollar ninety-nine."

My father and I start down the aisle. The wedding guests all turn to beam at us. "Or three pieces of chicken and two rolls for two ninety-nine," he adds.

"Let's not talk about chicken as we walk down the aisle," I say.

"Sure, honey," he says. "Plus tax."

I focus my gaze on Gabriel, my aristocratic cowboy. I'm walking to him, only him. My father is giving me away.

Gabriel's face lights up when he sees me in my bridal gown for the first time. He looks happier each step I take closer to him; I worry whether a person could actually burst with joy.

Finally my father and I stand before the hospital chaplain. "Who gives this woman in marriage?" the chaplain says. The church falls still.

Gabriel looks at me. I look at my father. Has he forgotten his line, if he ever knew it?

My father turns around to look for my mother. "I do," he says when he finds her. "And her mother does too."

The chaplain asks whether anyone present knows of any reason Gabriel and I should not be married. "Speak now," he says, "or forever hold y'all's peace."

The chaplain is used to dealing with people who've succumbed to spiritual eclecticism. In between the Bible passages, he tells us we'll share in the responsibilities and joys of life, in function and dysfunction. I hand my bouquet of white roses and gardenias to Gigi when the chaplain asks Gabriel and me to join right hands.

"Gabriel, do you take Colleen to be your wife?" the chaplain says. "Will you commit yourself to her happiness and self-fulfillment as a person and do you promise to love and honor her whether you're on call or not, as long as you both shall live?"

"I do," Gabriel says.

"I, Colleen, do promise and covenant with you, Gabriel, before God and these witnesses," I repeat after the chaplain, "to be your loving and faithful wife, downsized or employed, as long as we both shall live."

The chaplain bends down to unpin our rings from Gabe's pillow.

"Mine!" Gabe says in a loud voice. He plants his little hand over the rings.

"It's okay, Gabe," Gabriel says to him. "You did a great job."

We give each other our rings in token and pledge of our abiding love, with all that we have and all that we are.

"By the authority of God and the laws of the state of Texas," the chaplain says, "I declare Colleen and Gabriel are husband and wife."

Gabriel lifts my face veil, kisses me so passionately that the congregation gasps.

"You may kiss the bride," the chaplain says.

Gabriel kisses me again.

The chaplain is nonplused. "I now present to you Dr. and Mrs. Gabriel Benedict," he announces to thunderous applause.

We turn to face our family and friends. Gigi hands me my bouquet, rearranges my long train. Someone starts "the wave"; the guests rise and fall, row after row, as Gabriel and I walk together back down the aisle.

Peaches put her foot down when Gabriel and I wanted to have our reception in the hospital cafeteria. "It would be so convenient to the chapel," I said. "People wouldn't have to park twice." She arranged for us to have it in the ballroom at the Houston Country Club, through a sister Pi Phi. "Only my sorority sisters would come through for me in a crisis this big," she said.

My mother reluctantly stands first in the receiving line, the only receiving line she has ever been in. Peaches stands next to her, King next to Peaches.

"If my mother faints," I say to Gabriel, "we'll all fall like debutantes."

"Where should I stand?" my father says.

"Fathers in the receivin' line is optional," Peaches says.

"Right here would be lovely," I say. I place my father between King and me. The guests are supposed to be introduced down the line, but my mother doesn't know anybody. In no time, the guests are in chaos, the line in disarray. Peaches would blame this on my father, but he wins her over with anecdotes of his homelessness.

"I collect cans, sure," he says to her. "But the dumpsters aren't as good as they used to be."

"Where's Gabe?" Gabriel says.

Gigi's supposed to be watching him, but she's busy flirting. Barbara's frantic over Dusty, who bit a hole in his inflatable crib and crawled away. Through the crowd I see Gabe attack Gabriel's armadillo groom's cake with both hands. By the time we get to him, he's sitting under the head table. His little bare feet stick out from the white damask tablecloth.

"Where are your shoes?" I ask him. Felicity's not here, so they can't be in her purse.

"Don't take off anything else," Gabriel says.

Peaches worked for days on a precise seating plan for the hundreds of guests. Each got a tiny envelope with a table number. The women in my networking group started trading numbers, and now all the guests are doing it as if they're business cards.

"The ballroom looks like the floor of the Fort Worth Livestock Exchange," Gabriel says.

"Who's that?" Vanessa asks me. She nods at a handsome African-American man talking with my father, the two of them having the time of their lives.

"My homeless consultant!" I say. I'd left a wedding invitation for Chance with Georgia Balboni, but I was afraid I'd never see him again.

"I'm happy you change the behaviors causing you problems," Chance says when I rush over to him.

"Thank you for coming to our wedding," I say. "But what helped you?"

"God found me," he says.

Being found seems more to the point than finding God. "Then what?"

"He got me into a treatment program," he says. "He know everyone. He speak to us all the time, but we don't listen."

"How do we know it's God speaking?"

"If it's too hard, costs you money, and you don't want to do it," he says, "that's God."

The laughter of wedding guests rises and swells like a chorus.

My mother looks happier than I've ever seen her, if overwhelmed by Southern charm and Texan *joie de vivre.* "You're the first woman in our family to have a successful relationship," she says, the way people do about college graduation.

"Since when?" I say.

"The potato famine, at least," she says.

Robert and Sidney offer us their congratulations. "What are you serving?" Robert asks.

"Gourmet Texan cuisine," I say.

"That's an oxymoron." Sidney says.

But the club chef outdoes himself with a special menu of Texas rattlesnake pâté, cactus Hollandaise, buffalo Wellington, chicken-fried steak, mashed 'taters au gratin, and barbecued tofu for the vegetarians.

"Is chicken-fried steak," Doug says referring to a national food of Texas, "chicken fried like steak or steak fried by chickens?"

"Taste it," Gabriel says.

"I did," he says, "but I still can't tell."

"That's why Texas is a good place to be a vegetarian," I say.

Pamela congratulates us, tells me how happy she is I'm settled. "Men protect their investments," she says.

Chelsea crawls up to a plastic pink flamingo in a potted azalea. She pinches one of the pink petals between two fingers, then holds the flamingo's beak between her tiny hands and kisses it. Gabe doesn't know what to make of this.

King's toast includes a true story about the world's only married armadillos, Hoover and Starr. "If y'all don't believe me," he says, "check their marriage license in the county courthouse."

Gabriel toasts me and our parents. His hand on mine, we cut our wedding cake—the twelve-layered white cake decorated with marzipan magnolia blossoms. Covered with chocolate, Gabe can't accept that he has to share Gabriel's armadillo groom's cake.

"Someday, Gabe," Gabriel tells him, "this will all be yours."

The society country-and-western orchestra bursts into a western swing rendition of "Here Comes the Bride." Gabriel and I glide to the floor for our first dance, waltz across the ballroom. Everyone joins in when the orchestra segues into a two-step, followed by a western polka. We have a country-and-western dance teacher on hand to teach steps to the Yankees.

Peaches is horrified to hear I got my wedding gown at a shelter thrift shop.

"Lots of brides wear someone else's gown," Gabriel says.

"Those are heirlooms," she says.

"This is somebody's heirloom," he says. "We just don't know whose."

As a wedding gift, Peaches and King have commissioned a cattle mural of the Chisholm Trail for the western wall of Gabriel's condo.

"What china pattern did you register for?" Peaches says. "I hear y'all got a hundred place settings from our friends."

"Westward Ho's *Rodeo,*" I say. I fell in love with the lassooing cowboy in the center of the dinner plate.

"How's that going to look with your Grand Baroque silver and Tiffany crystal?" she says. "Why didn't you choose a traditional floral?"

"Not the Yankee way," I say.

"What do I say when my friends ask who *was* she?" Peaches asks Gabriel.

"Tell them she was a Sweeney, of the Boston Sweeneys," he says.

I'm the happiest I've ever been, at the sight of so many people I love having fun. Gabriel laughs with our guests, proudly introduces me as his bride. Gabe hovers near us, the three of us a triumvirate of love.

A hush descends over the single women who gather when it's time to toss my bouquet. The difficulty of finding a good man these days lends gravity to the proceedings.

"Yes!" Gigi says, when she catches it.

Gabriel removes my blue satin garter. One of Gabriel's doctor friends catches that. Gigi makes a beeline for him.

Our families gather around us to say their goodbyes. Each member of my family hugs me, shakes Gabriel's hand.

Peaches looks as if she has something important to tell me.

"What is it?" I ask, touched.

"Think about becomin' a blonde," she says. "People might accept you better."

"They might think I'm from California."

"Another couple of earthquakes, there won't *be* any blondes in California."

"I'll still have a Yankee face."

"Not if you rinse it enough the soap won't work cracks in it," she says.

"Wipe off your boots every time you wear them," King says. "So the dust won't work cracks into the leather."

"Give me some sugar, baby," Dalzenia says as she wraps Gabriel in a hug.

"Dalzenia," I say when I hug her. "You don't think Gabriel will be sorry he married me?"

"He a doctor," she says. "He certified in this, he certified in that. Baby, there ain't nothing wrong with you he can't fix."

I take Gabe into my arms. "You're my trophy stepson," I say.

"Colleen and I are going on our honeymoon," Gabriel says to Gabe as he hands him over to Peaches and King to take back to Felicity. "Do you know what that is?"

"You take your honey to the moon," he says.

Gigi's eyes are wet as she helps me and my dress into the back of the white limousine with the longhorn hood ornament. Gabriel climbs in the other side, puts his arm around me.

The driver discreetly starts the engine.

"I don't want to be anywhere else but here, with you," Gabriel says.

"I don't want you anywhere else, either."

He smiles at me in a way that's now familiar. It's not that he doesn't take me seriously. It's more like that of a non-directive therapist I once had, who smiled as if I were a practical joke his colleagues were playing on him, one he was determined to figure out.

But Gabriel looks like a man in the grip of something, not necessarily a great idea. "I love you so much," he says.

"I love you too," I say. I fall into the look in his eyes. "We're actually quite compatible in every way."

"Can I get that in writing?"

The hardest adjustment to being married to each other will be getting used to being happy. Gabriel's strong, but I am too. Why should I make that a problem?

"Where are we going on our honeymoon?" I say.

"The Ranch of Eden, right in the middle of Texas," he says. "More important, shall we make love the minute we get there?"

"How do we feel?"

"I asked us first," he says.